I0583166

THE LAST RESORT

By David Farrell

Copyright © 2014 by David Farrell

All rights reserved.

This book or any portion thereof may not be reproduced or used in any manner whatsoever without the express written permission of the publisher except for the use of brief quotations in a book review.

Printed in Australia.

First Printing 2018

ISBN 978-0-646-99319-5

Dedicated to the Cast & Crew of the

feature film The Last Resort

Thank you.

1.

As the morning light invited itself onto his face Rob immediately forgot his dream. He rolled over to shield himself and in the process partially crushed his erection. Celeste was still asleep with her lips parted slightly. Rob thought about kissing her but considered that his unshaven face might provoke a fight. The cream coloured pillowcases she purchased stared back at him. Celeste had gradually crept into his world and turned it upside down. Rob wouldn't have minded it except that now they had evolved into something else. He stared at her impotently and waited for his body to get on the same page as his mind.

Wake, Eat, Work, Sleep, Repeat.

He was a man on a mission. Today would be the final chance to work on the Trent report before the presentation next week. The alarm clock burst into song at 7.15am and he quickly stopped it and slipped out of bed to avoid waking Celeste. Since they started living together he was trying to be more considerate. Rob had found out the hard way many times during their relationship that she was a late riser. While showering he contemplated the best cereal to consume. Froot Loops was the stand out winner because while Celeste slept Rob could cheat on his diet and get away with it. He wasn't really *very* overweight. The annoying by-product of living together was that Celeste had watched him avoid fruit and vegetables too many times to ignore. She had thrown a massive tantrum once when he chewed his delicious sugary cereal too loudly in her presence. Rob had always considered himself to be average but Celeste could see the potential in him and was always pushing him to become his best self. She liked to joke that she was rebuilding him from the ground up. This dance had been tiring him lately. Today in her absence he could enjoy a break. The early hours of his day had become a time of relaxation and reflection for Rob. He read articles, returned emails and played Sudoku. This routine would always be broken the minute Celeste rose. Rob loved her, of course – but he had recently discovered he also loved Sudoku.

Celeste was sleeping lightly when the sound of a slamming door forced her hazel eyes to open. She felt as though she hadn't slept well in years. Celeste suffered from self-diagnosed anxiety. She had always over analysed everything and couldn't switch off her mind. This morning was no different. She lay on her side and listened to the man she loved drive away. Rob was gone. At the beginning of their relationship he wouldn't have left her if he didn't absolutely have to. They spent countless hours naked on his mattress discovering each other's bodies. This honeymoon period had shown Celeste the *real* Rob. He had let his guard down and she had fallen in love with him. It was unexpected. Her friends didn't understand it. Rob was certainly not the kind of guy she usually dated. Somehow they just clicked – or at least they *used* to. She took a moment and let her eyes land on his memory foam pillow.

As she started to worry about where he had gone she suddenly felt like the room was a hundred feet wide and that she was fading away. The note in their kitchen read simply *'Call you at lunch'* - which was unhelpful. It looked like it was written in haste. Celeste looked in the sink and saw a solitary green Froot Loop staring up at her. She shook her head, threw the Froot Loop into the bin and exhaled deeply. To calm herself down she would require a session of morning yoga. She unrolled her purple yoga mat and hoped her morning would improve.

Oblivious to Celeste's annoyance Rob had arrived at work and was proof reading the Trent report. It had recently been bound and looked extremely professional. He ran his fingers through his brown hair and smiled. Rob was chuffed and so far every detail was as he had imagined. Rob decided to reward himself. He opened an airtight bag in his drawer and removed a single cigarette from within. *Damn,* he thought knowing he would have to buy more for next time. His desk was the nearest to the courtyard which had led to a secret relapse for Rob. Celeste was disapproving for all the right reasons but Rob had naturally found a shred of rebellion in the act and took some pride in lighting up around co-workers so openly. Here he was 'Work Rob' – a rebel. Sure, he stuck to things like the IT policy but after finding out how many smoke breaks his colleagues were allowed to take it seemed an easy trade off. Smoking may cause lung cancer but ironically it was also the only time Rob got to go out for some fresh air during the day. This simple act would also result in many unproductive minutes of gargling mouthwash and disguising the scent.

Celeste must not find out.

Rob would be the first to admit he was stressed at work. He sat and stared at the oak tree in the courtyard. It was huge and he wondered whether the office had been built around it or whether it had been added afterwards. Maybe it was a rare or endangered tree that they couldn't cut down. Architects and builders were left scratching their heads until they came up with the courtyard concept. It stood in defiance of everything around it. Rob found it oddly inspiring. This upcoming presentation could solidify a pay increase for him and then perhaps he could afford to buy a house! Rob thought about how impressive that would be to Celeste. They had been offered the first rental they ever applied for together. Rob was nervous about living with Celeste at the start but he knew it had to happen sooner or later. He just thought it would be later. He finished his cigarette and returned to his desk enthusiastic about the future. A house was the dream and Rob was in the realm of making it come true. Before he could commence his post-cigarette cleaning regime his phone rang.

"Robert Miller speaking."

There was a pause before an icy tone responded, "It's me."

Concern filled Rob and he blurted out "Celeste, what is it? Are you *okay?*"

His head swam with frightening scenarios.

"I'm fine, I suppose."

And so begins another fight.

This was classic Celeste. She would offer no explanation as to why she was in a mood and Rob would have to decipher clues to figure out what he had done wrong. Even though Celeste was moody at times Rob knew that it was temporary. He was a lucky guy. Rob chose his words carefully, hoping the storm would pass quickly.

"I said I'd call you at lunch. I have a lot of stuff to do before then hon. Can this wait an hour?"

"Rob...its Saturday."

"...What?"

"You're at work and its Saturday."

Looking around Rob could see that all the other desks were empty. It was like a fog had been lifted. Why hadn't he realised this sooner?

Shit.

He tried to mask his surprise.

"Yeah... Celeste I have a lot of work to do...to catch up on, you know? I've been falling behind." Celeste was not amused by this attempt to smooth over the situation. She made a disapproving sigh and picked at the loose thread of her shirt.

"Is it me?"

Shit. Shit. Shit.

"What do you mean?"

"Is it something I said…. or did?"

"You? Of course not."

Wake, Eat, Work, Sleep, Repeat.

Fumes from Celeste could be felt down the phone line as she spoke.

"Then why did you run to work for the first time *ever* on a Saturday instead of staying with me on our nine month anniversary?"

SHIT.

…

Rob paused without any way of responding and Celeste quickly pounced.

"Oh…that's much better, you forgot!"

Although he was tempted to state that nine months wasn't a *real* anniversary that anyone celebrated experience told him to start doing damage control.

"Celeste, I'm so…so … I'm coming home, right now."

"Oh no, you have ALOT of work to do...you know...to catch up on?"

Rob found himself without any options.

"I'm coming home now..." he said as Celeste hung up the phone.

What do people give each other for their nine-month anniversary?

It had been a testing morning for their relationship. Neither of them could have imagined the chain of events that had been set into motion by that phone call.

2.

Rob cautiously entered their house with flowers in hand. The bouquet was made entirely by the woman at the flower shop so Rob had no idea what it contained. He had thought about ringing the doorbell but decided it was a weak move. This showdown had come out of nowhere but he hoped that it would be resolved quickly. Luckily Rob suddenly found himself with a day off. Celeste had positioned herself on the couch with arms crossed. She wore an oversized grey knit jumper over the top of her yoga clothes. Rob commenced grovelling before he had even shut the front door.

"I got these for you. I know I messed up but I'm here now. I'm all yours."

Celeste stood up and stared vacantly at Rob. She felt like the discarded toy of a toddler. Rob only wanted Celeste when it was convenient to him and she needed more than flowers to make amends this time.

"They're nice. Why don't you put them in a vase for me?"

She walked out of the room and headed upstairs leaving Rob completely confused. He dropped the flowers into a vase and followed her upstairs. In the heat of the moment he didn't even think about filling the vase with water. They had already begun to wilt.

Celeste was utterly fed up. She had started packing a black suitcase and the chaos of her wardrobe was spilling out onto the bed.

"You're leaving me? Come on Celeste be reasonable," he said in a state of continuing shock.

She spoke down to Rob as one might to a disobedient dog.

"Would you agree that you've made a *mistake*?"

Her inflection on the word 'mistake' had Rob worried. What would he have to do to fix things with Celeste?

"Of course and I'm sorry. Please, just stop packing," he pleaded.

Celeste continued tossing clothes and dresses in a pile but began to offer an olive branch. To her fighting was only an acceptable tactic if you won.

"I think you'll need to do more than apologise to fix this Rob."

"What then? How can I fix this?"

I'll do anything. Don't leave me. Please.

Celeste smiled knowing that Rob would fall into line. "Pack your suitcase. You're coming with me," she said with a sly smile.

Rob was completely lost. "Where are we going?"

"The mountains."

He hadn't expected an actual destination. Celeste had already decided they were going to the mountains?

"And how are we going to get there?"

"You're going to drive us."

Rob's mind was a mess of thoughts. It was Saturday and he could easily afford to take a trip north. The report was basically finished. Maybe the break would be the perfect thing to centre him for next week. The mountains were a scenic two hours away and there were a dozen or so resort options on the way to the snow. It was the closest option for a holiday and yet Rob had never taken her there. When they started renting they bought a book about New Zealand and told themselves that they would plan the perfect holiday. They didn't have enough money to go but through the act of planning they hoped to become inspired and get there together one day.

Maybe this can still be settled at home.

"Look, I know I messed up and I'm trying to make things right but I think you're overreacting a bit don't you?"

Overreacting?

As usual it was the wrong thing to say. Celeste stopped packing and stared right through him.

"We need to do something Rob," she said.

During the course of their nine months together Rob and Celeste had been on two trips. They had both been to the beach and had fallen within their first two months of dating. For seven months Celeste had longed for romance.

Where was the Rob she had fallen in love with?

"Here's the thing, either you pack yourself a suitcase and spend the long weekend with me in the mountains or I go by myself. How's *that* for overreacting?"

Rob had forgotten it was a long weekend. That would give them an extra day, which made it more appealing. He continued to negotiate with her. Relationships were all about negotiating for Rob.

"I'll go away with you okay? To the coast or something if you want. What are we going to do in the mountains?"

"Something? As opposed to nothing," Celeste seemed distant as she spoke, "which is what we are doing now."

"What are you saying?" he asked.

Rob loosened his tie. *Wake, Eat, Work, Sleep, Repeat.* This cycle was designed to bring them together in their own home. He could see the light at the end of the tunnel but Celeste wasn't on the same page. She was an artist by trade, a real bohemian girl. He tried to consider whether her paintings had been especially angry lately.

"What do you *think* I'm saying?" she said raising her voice.

Celeste was very good at deflection: answering a question with a question.

Rob swallowed and tried to address the issue at the centre of their problems. His voice was shaky and his heart rate had quickened.

"Are you unhappy?"

Celeste sensed his fear and anxiety and softened slightly. Was she unhappy? She had certainly been happier at the start of their relationship but she didn't want to break up with Rob, it had just become complicated. Celeste wanted to simplify things and get back to the way it felt before.

"Look, if you come with me, I'll know you stepped out of our boring routine and did something with me. Something just for me."

Celeste heard herself and corrected out loud.

"For *us*."

Rob took her hand and held it tightly. "Celeste, I don't want you to go."

She could tell that he didn't want to keep fighting. His touch calmed her down and she gave him a quick kiss on the lips.

"Then come with me."

All options for negotiation had been exhausted and Rob pulled his matching suitcase down. Celeste couldn't hide her smile as he began to pack. Celeste would wait until Rob had finished packing before she rewarded him with a proper kiss.

While filling up their overloaded hatchback with petrol Rob looked around. He couldn't see Celeste's eyes in the side mirror so he looked out at the horizon. As always he was having difficulty gauging her mood but was hopeful that she was cheering up. They were about halfway to the mountains now and conversation had started flowing more easily. Celeste had taken too long choosing her outfit but eventually landed on a black and white striped dress and red cardigan. This pit stop was more annoying to Rob than all the outfit changes. His car was a fuel-guzzling machine and even a short trip to the mountains was sure to require two tanks. It was mostly due to the fact that Rob demanded the most premium of fuel. He was sure it was the best thing for his car. Not every petrol station had the premium stuff and he was too fussy not to care. Stopping like this was also breaking up the conversation and Rob worried that he would have to start trying to impress Celeste all over again, as if a giant reset button was being hit each time they stepped away from each other. When he was done he reached down and felt the underside of his car. Rob kept a spare key in a magnetic box underneath the car and had a habit of making sure it was still there each time he got petrol. It was getting hot and the clouds were too thin.

Maybe I should buy sunglasses he thought to himself as he headed inside to pay.

While pacing the magazine section Rob considered purchasing a map. The attendant, a bored looking grease monkey, called out to him.

"Something you're looking for?"

He had shaggy blond hair and wore overalls that covered a Nirvana shirt.

"No, just…getting supplies."

He had noticed Rob looking at the maps and asked, "Where you headed?"

None of your business.

"Up to the mountains" Rob offered.

"Yeah? You and your girl there?" The attendant was leering out at Celeste. She was looking beautiful as the sun was hitting her in a very flattering way. She looked like a model in a sunglasses commercial.

"Yeah…"

Rob thought Celeste looked flawless except for the dark roots at the top of her otherwise light brown hair. There was no question she was the most beautiful woman Rob had ever dated. Even though the attendant was kind of creepy Rob decided he was happy with creating this envy.

That's right, she's with me he thought to himself proudly.

"Best be careful then. Drive safe."

Rob decided that both the map and the sunglasses were overpriced.

"Maybe you can give me some directions?"

The attendant seemed casual and finished his bottle of water before responding.

"Sure. Where you heading?"

"We're trying to get to Lake Cook resort."

Rob took the address from his pocket. The attendant (Gary according to his plain badge) looked at the paper and then at Rob.

"This place?"

"Yeah… I think so."

"You sure you wanna go here?" he said pointing at the address.

Rob was more intrigued than anything. He nodded and waited for an explanation.

"It's just… I thought this place closed down. If you booked it though…"

"Why would it close down?"

"No, it's nothing."

"So tell me?" Rob queried. They had definitely booked it. Rob hoped they hadn't been scammed online. Gary seemed equally intrigued. "I just thought it closed down because of the owner – but I guess I'm wrong huh?" He gave detailed directions to Rob and the remainder of the transaction was as expected. Rob made a mental note to Google the resort and its owner the next time he had phone reception.

A tiny bug landed on the dashboard of the car and immediately started struggling on the hot surface. Within a minute it had been overwhelmed by the heat and dropped dead. As the drive continued they approached a couple of hitchhikers by the side of the road. Rob had always had excellent vision and was able to see them far in the distance. The man was handsome and rugged with longer-than-most hair. He struck Rob as the outdoorsy kind of man. The kind of man who could pitch a tent and make fire using only two sticks. The woman was obviously very fit and Rob was careful not to be seen checking her out in front of Celeste. They both carried backpacks and had some kind of walking sticks. Rob wondered if there was a company that sold walking sticks exclusively and whether there was much of a market for them. Celeste nudged Rob and interrupted his debate on whether or not they needed a ride.

"It'll be all right you know."

"Yeah? How's that?"

"It's not like we're camping out in a tent you know. It's a resort. It's got activities and stuff."

Rob was still sceptical, as he hadn't seen any pictures of Lake Cook or the resort. He was trying to be receptive to it all but it went against his nature. The word *trust* kept floating into his mind and he smiled as optimistically as he could.

"Like?"

Celeste put her hand on his shoulder as she responded.

"Hiking?"

Did she mention hiking because she was checking out that hiker?

The truth was Celeste didn't particularly care about hiking but she couldn't remember all the activities off the top of her head. Rob looked over to the two hikers as they passed them. The girl was sticking out her thumb for a ride but Rob didn't slow down. Having another attractive girl around wasn't the kind of thing that would help Celeste get over their fight. He tried to keep the conversation going.

"Hmmm… What else?"

Celeste strained to remember the website.

"Canoeing? Swimming?"

Rob didn't get a lot of sunshine sitting in an office all week and knew he was paler than most. The idea of having sex with Celeste in a swimming pool created images that he couldn't get out of his mind.

"I dunno…" His eyes searched for something other than the repetitive expanse.

Celeste crawled her hand onto Rob's leg causing him to flinch suddenly. Affection was a very pleasant surprise.

Should I pull over?

"Ok, so we just need to find something more relaxing" she said.

"It would have been relaxing at home."

The hand was withdrawn. The fantasy changed and suddenly Rob was alone in the swimming pool.

That was the wrong thing to say.

"You and I both know that if we were home this weekend all you would do is catch up on work."

Though it may have been true Rob decided it was an assault and replied aggressively.

"What's wrong with that?"

"Work ends at 5pm. You should be happy you're not at work."

He thought about the house he was planning to buy and the future he was building for them both.

"I work hard."

"No argument here!"

What Rob struggled to say was that the reason he worked so hard was to make Celeste happy. He loved her very much but seemed to run into walls every time he tried to show her. Affection had never been his strongest suit and he blamed his divorced parents. He was so much like his father. Were the intimacy issues he had inherited destined to ruin his relationships?

"I love you but I don't know what you want from me."

It was a cliché but it was true. Men and women were different and sometimes it was enough to just find some common ground. Celeste could tell that he was making an effort and that was enough for now.

"Thank you for coming."

Rob felt satisfied with that response. He wondered if he could still make his swimming pool fantasy come true this weekend. If he had any sex this weekend all this effort would be worth it.

Shoot for the moon. Even if you miss, you'll land among the stars.

Up ahead an abandoned red car sat by the side of the road. It had a flat tyre and Rob wondered if it belonged to the two hikers. He decided that if it did they would reach the petrol station shortly where Gary would surely be able to help them.

3.

Rob had only just noticed the layer of dirt under his fingernails. It must have been there for hours but he just hadn't looked at them. There had been other things on his mind. It had been a long time since Rob arrived at the police station and had been ushered into this interrogation room. There was no clock in the room but Rob had felt every minute. He kept staring at the dark dome on the ceiling, knowing that somewhere he was being watched. The door opened from the outside unless you had a swipe card.

It was an extremely boring white room and he had nothing to do but collect his thoughts. By the time the door opened Rob had his head in his hands. Constables Lawsov and Wilkins entered the room. In their time at this regional station they had seen all types of criminals sitting in that chair but Rob represented new territory. They would have to figure out what he'd done. It was crucial that they get to the bottom of what happened at the resort. Wilkins spoke first. To Rob he appeared to be the older and wiser of the two.

"Sorry we kept you waiting…" he checked his clipboard "…Rob."

It was a power move. Wilkins had been researching interrogation techniques and was thrilled to have someone other than his wife to practice them on. He made sure to remain standing to assert his dominance over Rob.

"I've been sitting here for nearly four hours."

Wilkins flipped through the pages on the wooden clipboard while Lawsov sat down opposite Rob. Rob thought it was strange to have a wooden clipboard and hadn't seen one in years. This relic represented everything Wilkins loved. He was an analogue man in a digital world. Lawsov stared daggers at Rob. He was wearing his most expensive dark grey suit, which was impressively tailored to his physique.

"You're not even going to give me some excuse about why I've been waiting?" Rob cried angrily.

Wilkins tried to pause for as long as possible before replying. He managed to mask the fact that he was enjoying work for the first time in a month. People didn't turn up dead in regional Australia as often these days as they used to.

"We've been following up your initial statement. This is my colleague Constable Lawsov." He intentionally didn't give his name.

Let me be the mysterious one he thought happily.

Lawsov looked as though he may have a military background based on his haircut and demeanour. He was certainly not a policeman you would run from.

"Afternoon."

Rob noticed that Lawsov hadn't blinked since he entered the room. It made him uneasy which he assumed was the point. Wilkins continued the interrogation and spoke in measured sentences.

"Listen I have some more questions. I just need you to tell your story to Constable Lawsov. Just to check some… facts."

When he first arrived Rob had spoken to an inept rookie at the front desk. Everything he said overwhelmed the man and he was asked to write it all down. After he complied he found himself an unwilling prisoner for the second time that weekend. He never should have gone to the mountains with Celeste. This was beyond frustrating for Rob and he wondered why they hadn't come in to see him sooner. Maybe they were out to lunch.

"I've already told you what happened. It's all there in my statement. Did you read it? Don't you believe me?"

"We just want to be sure. Would you mind telling us again?" Wilkins asked politely.

Lawsov remained silent but picked up the clipboard as if he had never seen it before. *Maybe they hadn't even read the statement.*

"To be honest, yes, I would mind. I've told you about the murders and I've been sitting here waiting for too long."

Lawsov began writing something down while Wilkins continued.

"Listen Rob humour me here. I just need to get my facts straight and then we can talk about what's going to happen next."

Rob was sporting a three-day growth and it had started to itch. He was used to order and routine – part of which included shaving on a daily basis. He was exhausted in every way possible but knew that he had to press on.

Let's just get this over with.

"Well…what do you want to know?"

"What were you doing at Lake Cook resort?"

Seriously?

"Everything you need to know is right there in my statement."

Lawsov finally blinked and decided to join in on the questioning.

"If you wouldn't mind, we're going to need to hear it again."

"I came here to report the murders…"

Rob was stressed. He could feel his neck itching more and more. He couldn't help it and started scratching. Wilkins suppressed a smile. He was sure this would be the 'tell' that gave it all away. The interrogation research was working a charm. He fantasised about Rob breaking down in tears and confessing to it all. The thought was so delectable that he momentarily covered his mouth to avoid giving his glee away.

"How many *murders* again Rob?"

Lawsov was still like a lion waiting for a gazelle to move within range. When Rob didn't immediately respond he continued with a note of sarcasm to his speech.

"Why don't you just repeat what you wrote earlier?"

While Lawsov was become annoying Rob found himself watching Wilkins. Wilkins reminded Rob of his father. He probably had some almost grown up kids at home and this interrogation was keeping him from having dinner with them. Rob had never really known his father. He was an introvert and had always had his head in a book.

"Did you kill them Rob?" Lawsov asked, ignoring his instincts and playing bad cop.

"No..." he said looking at Wilkins.

Lawsov began writing again.

Is he just writing the word 'no' down?

Rob was too tired to process the movement of the pen. Wilkins produced a bag of throat lozenges from his breast pocket and popped one into his mouth.

"Let's go over this again."

Rob felt his whole body clench with frustration.

4.

Rob and Celeste looked at the sign as they turned off the highway and down a weathered track.

LAKE COOK RESORT.

The lettering was silver on black. They had finally arrived. Rob assumed the resort and the lake in the middle of it were named after Captain James Cook. It was a safe bet as there weren't many famous Cooks he could think of. It was isolated but seemed well maintained. Rob couldn't help but think of the exchange with Gary at the service station and wonder why he thought this place had closed down. As they drove along the gravelly road past large rocks Celeste was sure she saw a brown snake. A voice inside her head told her not to tell Rob because she didn't want to give him any excuses.

We are going to have a great time she told herself.

She had grown up absolutely sure that the glass was always half full. In recent years she needed to remind herself more and more. Had she been naïve? Had her image of love been based on the films of her youth? She had been burnt in relationships before but she kept hoping each time for the real deal. If you start a relationship thinking it will go wrong then it inevitably does.

The reception was a ghost town. Small weathered metal statues of kangaroos stared at Celeste as she unbuckled her seatbelt. The weather was perfect except for a mess of ominous grey clouds in the distance.

"Okay, I'll go get the room key if you wanna grab the bags?" Celeste said. She wanted to get into the rooms, dump the bags and explore their new surroundings as soon as possible. Rob's bladder had other ideas.

"Okay, I just need a pit stop."

"Meet you back here?" she said indicating to the picnic area as she started towards reception.

"Alright."

There was a wooden outdoor bathroom near the picnic area and Rob wandered in. Standing on a stepladder changing a light bulb was a tall man in a kind of khaki uniform. Rob couldn't see his face as he moved past him towards the urinal. He stood there, penis in hand, unable to urinate. He looked back over his shoulder and felt as though he was being watched. Having this man on a stepladder above Rob was strangely unnerving and he was temporarily frozen.

"You okay down there?" a bold voice echoed.

Rob returned his member to the safety of his pants and quickly moved to the sinks.

"Yep, fine. Don't need to go after all."

I can hold it a bit longer.

Washing his hands he was able to use the mirror to get a good look at the employee. He had defined features that all worked together to compliment his face. The man had piercing blue eyes and an enviable jaw line. As he got caught staring at him Rob felt he had to say something before it became awkward. Eye contact in the men's bathroom could be easily misinterpreted.

"Do you work here?"

Dumb question as he is changing a light bulb.

"What? Here in the bathroom?" he joked. Rob did not get it or at least failed to see it as a joke at all.

"I mean at the resort."

"Yes. Why? Do you need help with your bags?"

Although the man was still joking Rob took it as a genuine offer.

"Come to think of it, that would be good."

Celeste had packed multiple bags for this short trip and Rob figured at least this way he wouldn't have to carry them all. This kind of laziness had become one of Rob's less flattering qualities. Unfortunately he was oblivious to how this was affecting Celeste. It just seemed to her as if he was less romantic and less interested than he had first appeared.

"Just let me finish this?" the man said holding up another light bulb.

"Oh sure… I'll wait."

Rob wondered if he was doing any long-term damage as he did his best not to think about peeing.

Celeste was impressed with the reception area. As she walked in she was greeted by a giant painting of a shipwreck. The detail delighted Celeste and she took a moment to study it. The whole space had been decorated with realistic looking artefacts from the time of Captain Cook. There were miniature ships and inkpots at the desk. Celeste picked up a quill and started to sign the guest book. She was so focussed on all the knick-knacks that she went right past the reception desk where an old man was sitting.

"You must be Celeste Cooper?" he said with a knowing smile.

Celeste stopped suddenly when she heard her name.

"Yes..."

"I'm Thomas. You must be here to check in."

Celeste squinted slightly and noticed a light discolouration in his eyes. He was alternating between looking into the distance and down at the desk.

"How did I know, right?" Thomas said.

Celeste made a noise that she had never made before and had no idea what it meant. Luckily Thomas ignored it, which kept the conversation going.

"You're the only one with a booking."

"Oh right!" she said sighing with relief.

It was a beautiful looking resort and Celeste felt lucky to be the only one with a booking.

It was strange that no one else had decided to come here on a long weekend but that meant no lines for the restaurant and a private pool to swim in. Celeste was quite content now and felt her glass half full attitude coming back.

"You sound trustworthy, why don't you pick a room?" said Thomas indicating to the numbered cards hanging on the wall.

"Oh no…that's okay." Celeste responded timidly.

"They're all empty. Go on. Any one you like."

"I'd rather not."

This is odd behaviour.

"Well I can't do it for you."

"Excuse me?"

"I'm sorry to say that I'm quite blind. I don't usually sit at the reception desk. I'm just here in case the phone rings while some light bulbs are being changed."

Celeste felt suddenly stupid for not putting it together. She was always putting herself in awkward situations like this.

"I'm so… sorry. I didn't even realise!"

It was obvious now that she looked closer. Thomas's eyes were looking through her and she could see him using his ears to confirm her position.

"Think nothing of it. A room for two right?"

Celeste nodded and then quickly added "Please."

"So which room would you like to stay in?" Thomas asked with another smile.

The cards all looked the same and Celeste assumed the rooms would be too. She picked her birthday.

"Room 14?"

"14. You're sure now?"

"Yes."

Thomas stood up and silently counted his way along for the fourteenth card. Celeste determined he was probably in his late sixties or early seventies. While he was a nice enough man it seemed very impractical for him to work here. What did he do around here? She wondered whether he owned the resort.

Rob wandered out of the bathroom ahead of his new friend. He spotted Celeste leaning against the car and paced towards her. She had activity brochures in hand and Rob let out a sigh. This weekend was happening whether he liked it or not. He decided to smile and put on a brave face. He was never going to get any action this weekend if she thought he was moping about it. Celeste beamed at him. She looked beautiful as always.

"Got a key. One for you too."

"Why do we need two keys? Are we going to be splitting up?"

Celeste had noticed multiple times during their relationship that Rob liked to try and pre-empt their breakup. Rob had a history of being dumped and he was constantly expecting that what he had was too good to be true instead of enjoying it while he could. As a result he had made himself quite bitter when it came to matters of the heart. His lack of confidence in their relationship was one of the things Celeste hated most.

"Do you have separation anxiety or something? No, we're not splitting up. I just didn't want you to feel left out."

Also Thomas gave me two keys and I didn't want to question him.

Celeste was being sweet and it was very endearing to Rob. He liked her reassurance.

"Better be a good room," he mumbled to himself, forgetting his promise to seem happy.

"You going to carry the bags?" Celeste asked.

"Yeah... I..."

Rob turned and realised that they were alone. He had been ditched and would have to carry the bags himself.

What an asshole. He was never going to carry the bags at all.

"That's…weird…There was a guy here before."

"Are you sure?"

"Yeah I'm sure. I met him in the bathroom."

Celeste pulled a face. She hadn't seen anyone.

"We're the only ones with a booking."

"No, he said he worked here…"

Celeste didn't really believe him. She started to wonder when her doubts about Rob had set in. Did she still trust him? If the answer was no then she should know by the end of this trip. This weekend would be a test. Celeste liked testing people. She was also secretly hoping Rob would pass.

"Well, *I* don't see anyone."

Rob remembered what Gary had said at the petrol station. What was going on here?

"Wait, we're the only ones with a booking?"

"Yeah."

Filled with new doubts Rob was questioning everything. "Maybe we're at the wrong place then."

This was a ridiculous statement as they had clearly seen the name of the resort on the drive in. He was getting under her skin now.

"What are you *talking* about?"

"Maybe there's a better and more popular resort down the road."

Celeste thought about the mountain views. She looked out at the serenity of the lake and the inviting scenery. She could taste the difference in the quality of the air here.

I'm not going anywhere. This is where we need to be.

"I think this weekend… we'll need the privacy."

Celeste kissed Rob passionately, taking him by surprise again.

Maybe this weekend is going to be ok after all.

"Now grab my bags."

5.

The room was dressed in the same colonial style as the reception was. They had their own inkpot and smaller guest book as well as a large ship in a bottle on the kitchen bench. It was overlooking Lake Cook and their balcony was equipped with a small heater. As it was the middle of summer this wouldn't be necessary but Celeste thought it was a nice touch. The living room had another oversized portrait, this time of a naval captain. It loomed above the sofa and his eyes seemed to follow guests around the room. Rob put his keys down on the glass coffee table.

"This will do I guess," Rob said as he tried the lights. "Huh…no power."

"You've got to put the card in," Celeste teased.

She expertly slid the card into the holder next to the light and the power hummed on.

Rob had been temporarily distracted by Celeste and finally escaped to the bathroom. Celeste was too busy thumbing through brochures to notice that he was peeing for the second time in ten minutes.

Feeling relieved he suddenly thought of the Trent report.

"This makes me wish I'd brought my laptop," he called as he washed his hands.

"We came here to forget about work, remember?" she shouted in return.

Rob had a sudden lapse in judgement.

"That's easy to say when you don't have a job."

Celeste was a painter and for years had loved selling her art and surviving from the sale of her work. She was never rich but always able to make ends meet. She decided that she would try and take photos of the landscape here with the goal of painting when she returned home. It would have been hypocritical of her to pack her paints since she gave Rob such a hard time about it being their weekend.

I'll take pictures for later she promised herself. She started unpacking her bag methodically.

Rob looked around the room stopping at the inkpot and quill. Having never used one before he wondered how difficult it was to write with and decided to try it out. After some effort he completed his name and returned the quill to the inkpot. He wandered over to Celeste in the bedroom.

"What are you doing?" asked Rob.

"What does it look like?"

"Don't unpack."

"Why?"

"Cos...we're on holiday."

"And?"

"Well, when you're on holiday you just live out of your suitcase so you never need to unpack it. If anything you should be putting more into it! Free bath towels and shampoo and all of that."

Rob could be very frugal. Celeste rolled her eyes.

"Seriously, they expect for that kind of thing. They account for it in their budgets and yearly projections."

"This sounds a lot like work talk to me."

Sometimes it felt to Rob as though every conversation was leading towards a fight.

She's going to leave me.

"I'm just making a point."

"The reason I'm unpacking is so my clothes don't become too creased and I can wear what I want without worrying about ironing."

There is no one else staying here, thought Rob, *so no one will care if your clothes are creased!*

Rob was sick of fighting so he didn't tell Celeste what he thought. He decided instead to make a play for intimacy. The kiss at the car had been playing on his mind.

"You look great no matter what you have on."

"Well, now you know the reason."

Rob took Celeste by the hips and turned her around to face him. It took her by surprise and she literally dropped her clothes to the floor. The unpacking would have to wait.

"No, Celeste…you're beautiful."

Celeste's lips found themselves firmly against Robs. She enjoyed the feeling of being held by him. She wondered how he always smelt so good.

"Thank you. That's sweet," she managed when she was able to catch her breath.

Rob smiled and kissed her again, more passionately this time, and started to edge them both towards the bed.

"Stop."

Celeste had picked up his intentions and wasn't ready to forgive him quite yet.

"Why not?"

You have to earn it again. Make me trust you.

"That's not why we're here."

He had hit another wall and it was just plain frustrating. He tried to argue his case.

"Wait, you said we needed to 'do something.' And here I am trying to make it happen – and you're saying no?"

For Celeste this trip really wasn't about sex. She had decided that this weekend represented a choice for her. Their relationship – heck their friendship - had been strained lately and this trip would either make or break them. Celeste wanted someone who loved her and always would. She didn't want to settle for Rob just because she would be turning thirty soon.

"I want you to remember why we are together, you know? Why are you going out with me?"

Celeste thought about all the men she had been with. There had always been a reason to end it. Each time they did something to confirm it was over. Was she asking too much of him? Was it really so difficult to spend time with her? Things had turned too serious for Rob. His face was scrunched closed as if he was trying to block her words.

"Okay…I'm going for a walk," he said while backing away. "Just to check the place out."

As he started to turn he noticed that three of his fingers had been stained with dark ink. He also realised that he had carelessly transferred some of that ink to Celeste when he grabbed her. Her top was probably ruined but he decided to stay silent.

Rob walked around with only his thoughts for company. The resort was bathed in sunlight as magic hour approached and everything glowed. It smelt different out in the mountain air. Rob noted that each of the cabins in the distance had the same shape and colour scheme. He wondered how expensive it would be to buy one. A cabin in the mountains would be useless most of the year but it would prove profitable in winter with its proximity to the snow. He had palmed his cigarettes from work and pondered whether he could get away with having one now. He didn't have his mints, deodorant or mouthwash on him so he would be running the risk of another confrontation. The water was still on the lake and he found a small bridge that crossed at its most shallow point. Rob produced a cigarette from his small plastic bag and lit it. He decided he could shower when he returned to the room and use the excuse of it being a long drive. Ducks happily waded past and Rob paused to watch them. It was at that moment, with his head bowed down, that a tap on the shoulder shocked him. It was the employee from the bathroom. In the light of day Rob saw how physically intimidating he was.

"Oh sorry!" he said realising that he had caused Rob to drop his cigarette into the lake. Rob's heart was racing and he was just thankful it wasn't Celeste.

"Jesus... It's all right. I thought you were someone else."

"What? Like your wife or something?"

Rob imagined being married to Celeste and always being in a fight. Sometimes when they hadn't had sex in a while he liked to joke that it was like they were already married. Being with her made him feel important as if he had somehow won the game of life. She was beautiful and he was surely the envy of many men. Rob had always thought he would eventually get married anyway. Maybe telling Celeste he was thinking about that kind of commitment would be enough to have sex with her later.

"She's not my wife."

"Sorry about before by the way. I remembered I had some other maintenance to do."

"That's okay."

Jerk.

"I'm Gordon by the way."

"Rob."

The two shook hands and Rob drew another cigarette from his bag.

"Mind if I bum a smoke?" Gordon asked while analysing Rob's method of carrying his cigarettes around.

"Sure."

Gordon nodded appreciatively and lit both of their cigarettes with a lighter of his own. Rob held his cigarette between ink stained fingers and took a long drag.

"I bet it was her idea to come, hey?"

"Yeah it was."

Rob assumed this must have been the case with most couples coming to this resort.

"Well I don't blame her, its beautiful here. Just look at that sunset."

The sunset was in full swing now and Rob and Gordon stood side by side silently watching the full sun descend. Unknown to either of them Celeste was taking pictures of the same sunset from their balcony though they were obscured from her view. Gordon could tell that Rob was distracted and gave him a little nudge with his elbow.

"You've got something else on your mind huh? Wanna tell me?"

Fuck off guy.

"I'm sorry I don't think that's any of your business."

"I don't mean to pry. I'm just glad you had cigarettes."

Rob shrugged and mumbled, "You caught me."

Gordon took another drag and leaned across the edge of the railing. He was a calming influence on Rob because he was the first person he'd seen in a while that wasn't trying to pick a fight.

"Well, if you need to talk about it… my ex always said I was a good listener."

Rob looked down as the ash from Gordon's cigarette fell and almost landed on top of the ducklings.

"Uhuh… thanks."

"See I figured one day I must *not* have been listening… and that's why I lost her.

So! In an effort to prove I'm a changed man I'm here to lend an ear."

"It's not a big deal."

"If it's not a big deal you can tell me. You don't want to be here?"

Rob was annoyed about being shot down earlier but now at the forefront of his mind it was the activities that seemed daunting to him. He didn't want to paddle a canoe or run through tall grass. The idea that Celeste was planning their weekend with those brochures made him want to jump in the lake.

"I'm not sure the outdoors are my thing. Do you get a lot of that here?"

"We get all types of people, from broken hearted to honeymooners. Everybody needs to get away from it all."

"But there's no one else here right now?"

"We were almost full the other week," Gordon stated matter-of-factly.

Weird.

Gordon finished his cigarette and stubbed it out with his foot. Rob had been standoffish and Gordon *did* mean to pry, even though he promised the contrary.

"So can I ask you a personal question?"

And the prying continues.

"I guess."

"Do you love her?"

Gordon held his gaze and it made Rob feel very uncomfortable.

You shouldn't ask people you've just met these kinds of questions.

"What?"

"You either do or you don't. It's none of my business I suppose."

Rob agreed that it wasn't any of his business but felt some primal need to impress Gordon.

"Ok, I love her, so what's your point?"

"There's your answer then." Gordon paused and took a moment to gauge Rob's reaction. Rob could see the same envious look that Gary had. Men seemed impressed by Rob *because* he was with Celeste.

Is Celeste the best thing about me? Rob wondered to himself.

"Listen, I'm going bushwalking tomorrow morning through the mountains."

Rob nodded and raised his eyebrows feigning interest.

"Why don't you bring your girl along and I can show you the sights," pressed Gordon.

Activities.

"I dunno."

Gordon had a way of getting what he wanted and changed his pitch slightly hoping to entice Rob.

"It's just walking around the mountain… around the lake… it's not an uphill *hike*. And besides, she'll think it's romantic. Trust me."

Rob had been looking for a way to inject some romance into this trip and this might just work. For some reason Rob saw Gordon as a trustworthy guy, despite not helping with the bags.

I'd rather walk around a lake than paddle across one.

"Let me run it by her."

"Oh sure…that's fine. Listen, if you *do* want to go, I'll be ready at eight, and I'll wait for you down over there. Near that tree?"

He pointed at a tree line clustered with all kinds of trees making it completely impossible to tell which one he meant.

"Yes, I see it" Rob lied as he finished his cigarette and stubbed it out.

"Great. Maybe I'll see you two tomorrow then?"

"Maybe."

"Thanks for the cigarette."

They were not completely alone at the resort. Gordon seemed a little too interested in Celeste and their situation. Rob skipped stones into the lake for a few minutes before it got too dark and he headed back to his girlfriend.

6.

Celeste was watching TV when Rob entered room 14. She had changed into sweatpants and he could see she was ignoring him.

"What are you watching?" he asked, genuinely interested.

"Nothing."

"You almost never watch TV… is this what you do when you're on holiday?"

"I can do what I like."

Celeste was annoyed that the deep and meaningful conversation they were about to have had been interrupted. It was getting easier to stay mad at Rob and that was a sad sign of the state of things between them.

Rob forgot about the cigarette smell as he cautiously moved to sit next to Celeste. Sensing her mood he tried to tread lightly.

"I want us to work things out. Speaking of which… do you have any plans for tomorrow?"

"Nothing comes to mind."

Celeste had lots of ideas from the brochures but wanted to see where he was going with this.

"That's good, because I ran into that guy that works here and he offered to take us on a hike tomorrow morning."

"A hike? Are you sure *you* want to do that?"

"Well, he assured me it would be a lot easier than a hike."

Rob smiled for a moment before remembering he had a mouth like an ashtray.

"Sounds pretty good," she beamed. Celeste was glad he had suggested it.

'Well, that's our morning planned. Anything else you have in mind for this weekend?' Rob asked while trying not to breathe in her general direction.

"Guess we will have to wait and see how the hike goes."

Celeste was flirting again, which was a great sign. Rob stood up and made his way to the bathroom.

"I'm going to go take a shower."

Celeste considered whether she should join him but remembered this weekend wasn't meant to be about sex. She changed the channel a few times but kept picturing Rob naked. She hopped out of her chair and grabbed their shared toiletry bag. Without thinking she took it into the bathroom and started unpacking its contents. She opened the mirrored medicine cabinet and took a cheeky glance at her man. He had noticed her come in but was trying to play it cool. Unfortunately his mind raced with ideas and his penis gave his intentions away. She closed the cabinet and felt her cheeks turn red. Celeste placed her electric toothbrush next to his plastic blue one. They were so different but they fit together so well. She paused at the sink and fantasised about stripping down to nothing and having sex with Rob in that shower. It would be so easy and she knew he would love it too. But then it would be over.

This weekend is not about sex - it's about love she reminded herself. Sex had become intertwined with love and now she wasn't sure if this felt right anymore. She turned around to face Rob and their eyes met. Celeste was glad there was a glass barrier between them.

"I'll get the dinner on," she said with a smile and bounced out of the bathroom.

A dinner of satay chicken had been eaten on the balcony and Celeste now sat quietly opposite Rob. Neither wanted to talk but the silence had grown uncomfortable and she decided she should see what was on his mind besides sex.

"It's beautiful here at night isn't it?"

"It's very different to the city. How did you hear about it?"

"I don't remember. I think someone told me they came here years ago and it just kind of stayed with me."

Rob put his feet up on the spare chair. They were overlooking the lake, which lapped small waves against the wall of their cabin. It seemed like the moon existed only to provide this place with light as it danced on the surface of the lake.

"Do you want dessert?" Rob asked.

"Not for me," Celeste replied.

"We still have all that yoghurt to eat."

They had stopped off and gotten a few supplies in a small town store before reaching their destination.

Why isn't he talking to me? Celeste wondered. *This doesn't feel right.*

Rob put his empty plate on top of Celeste's and leaned back in the chair.

He's crazy if he thinks I'm clearing those plates.

"Enjoying yourself?" he asked.

There was a tone to his question that Celeste wasn't sure of. It was like a challenge in disguise. She had chosen the resort so it was up to her to make it a fun holiday. If it went wrong it would be her fault because she dragged him here.

"Of course. This seems like a nice place for a family holiday."

Celeste had never talked to Rob about children and scrutinised his face as he responded.

"We're the only ones with a booking so how good can it really be."

"Well we can check it out when we go on that hike. I'd like to take a proper look around."

Rob had seen the restaurant as they'd driven in but had been careful not to mention it yet. It would be his 'ace in the hole' should the hike prove less romantic than Gordon had promised. Rob assumed it would be nice and tranquil and that Celeste would say she loved it even if she didn't. Gordon had disappeared once and could surely make himself scarce again after their walk.

"What else do you want to do this weekend?" Rob asked hopefully.

"Just spend time together," she replied. "I feel like we haven't done much of that lately."

"We haven't done much of anything lately."

It just slipped out.

"It's always about sex with you isn't it Rob?"

"No… that's not what I meant."

"Sex isn't everything you know."

"I know."

"Then why do you keep bringing it up?"

Rob resisted the urge to make a joke about 'bringing it up' and instead shrugged.

"I love you."

It was a response that Celeste had heard a lot of. It was Rob's go-to phrase whenever he had done something wrong.

"Sometimes love isn't enough," Celeste said. She meant it too. Their relationship had been relying on the fact that they loved each other alone. Romance had gone out the window. Celeste remembered the flowers Rob had brought home and correctly assumed they would be dead by now given the fact that they had both forgotten to put them in water. Their relationship was dying. Sex had become the furthest thing from Celeste's mind.

"Let's just clean up and go to bed." Celeste said.

I'm tired of fighting with you.

Rob thought this was a good sign and eagerly scooped up the dishes.

He lay awake in bed next to Celeste. She hadn't been affectionate that evening which had ended in a brief kiss and little else. Rob decided to stroke her back. He received no response so he nuzzled closer and started to kiss her on the back of the neck. The hot weather meant that neither of them had worn much to bed that night so Rob had access to more skin than usual.

"Rob, save your strength for the hike."

Celeste was barely awake.

"C'mon Celeste… I'm going crazy over here."

"Not tonight Rob, I'm tired."

Isn't this why we came here? he thought to himself, *we haven't had sex in days.*

Rob held Celeste for a moment and then bit her earlobe gently.

"I can wake you up…"

"No Rob."

She's half asleep. She doesn't know what she's saying.

Rob slid his hand down Celeste's side and into the front of her satin shorts. He held his breath as he moved slowly downward. Rob was getting excited and Celeste could tell.

"No is a complete sentence" she said.

He was so close. Reluctantly he removed his hand, lingering on her hip and then her side. He contemplated taking matters into his own hands for a moment before realising the mood had been spoiled.

"Night Celeste."

She didn't respond.

The mattress was moving when Rob opened his eyes. Celeste was already dressed in short shorts and a black tank top with her hair tied back in a ponytail. She sat on the edge of the bed and was partially silhouetted by the sunlight. Rob squinted at her through his fingers. Celeste threw her leg over him and positioned herself perfectly against his groin.

Where was this Celeste last night?

She leaned down and gave him a quick peck on the lips as though the events of last night had never occurred.

"Morning."

"Good morning" Rob crackled in his morning voice.

"C'mon get up. We have a hike to attend."

"Uh… No… Can't we stay here a bit longer?" he pleaded.

They were probably already running late. He wasn't even certain Gordon would show.

"No, no, no, mister. Get up."

"I am up," he mumbled to himself.

Celeste thought about seeing him in the shower and shook the image from her mind.

"We are going on this hike. It was your idea!"

"Uh… okay, okay. I'm awake."

Rob looked at his mobile phone. It was getting only one bar of service here in the mountains and was almost out of battery. He plugged it in and placed it on the carpet under the bed rather than on the bedside table. He didn't want Celeste to accuse him of trying to work on their holiday again.

With no time for a shower Rob found himself walking out the door in cargo shorts and a deep blue shirt.

He didn't own a lot of outdoor clothes and these would have to do.

"Where to then?" pestered Celeste. She was letting Rob lead the way and it felt good. He wasn't much of a leader and it had been a theme throughout his life. Rob had been in the same job for years. It was a decent wage but he definitely lacked ambition. Celeste had always wanted a man who was passionate about something. Rob was definitely passionate about her but seemed to lack other dimensions.

"We've got to head down to that tree. The guy said he'd meet us there."

Rob motioned to the tree line but still had no idea which tree Gordon had meant. She could see in his posture that this was a real effort and she loved him for trying.

"Are you having a good time yet?"

"No."

He surprised her with his response.

"Oh! No?"

"That's right."

"Not even right now?"

"The company is good."

Rob was hiding something and that made Celeste determined to find out more.

"But?"

Rob screwed up his face as he answered.

"I'm regretting the idea of hiking a little bit," he admitted.

"It means a lot to me that you're here."

Celeste linked arms with Rob.

"Well, feel free to show me how much it means to you later."

I get it. You want to have sex.

"Ha ha. You're so funny," Celeste said as she gave Rob a playful nudge in the ribs.

"Funny looking?"

"Not a bit."

She found herself picturing him in the shower again. She tried to focus on the bad parts of his body this time. Rob was pale but maybe all this hiking would result in a tan. His shoulders were broad and his arms were well defined but his jawline was almost non-existent. She started thinking about the conversation at dinner. They had almost talked about kids.

Do I want my children to have his undefined jawline? She freed her arm from his and let it fall to her side. They reached a tree and Rob leaned against it.

This tree will do.

Celeste watched Rob as he looked out over Lake Cook. He was a pretty great guy sometimes and there was a lot Celeste loved about him. She hoped that this weekend would show her the version of Rob she had fallen in love with nine months ago.

This trip will bring us closer together she decided as she folded her arms in front of her.

"I love you Rob."

"Love you too."

That's right. We're in love.

"Hey, what's the time?"

"It's after eight."

"So he's running late?"

Maybe he's not coming. Did he forget?

"I'm sure he's just..."

THUNK.

Suddenly without warning a thin red dart whizzed past Celeste and lodged itself into the side of Rob's neck. Celeste's eyes widened as she watched him tighten in pain and fall to his knees. The dart had a clear liquid inside it and whatever it was affected Rob immediately. She screamed as he collapsed onto the grass with his eyes rolling back in his head. Celeste was panicking and looked in every direction for their attacker. There were ample hiding places for a potential shooter and Celeste wasn't sure which direction the dart had come from. Celeste leaned down to check on Rob and a split second later a dart struck the tree near her head.

Holy Shit!

Celeste started running as survival instincts kicked in. She tore past Rob and down the slope near the edge of the lake. Celeste was not an athlete but as adrenaline kicked in she momentarily felt like one. She decided she wouldn't turn around until she reached the taller trees as they offered the best shelter.

What the hell is going on?

Being pursued was a horrible feeling and Celeste could sense herself being overwhelmed with fear. She tried not to cry as she cut through the mountain air and towards the trees.

Is he still alive? Is he dead?

There was no time to think about that now. The ground was riddled with roots and it wasn't long before she tripped on one. Celeste hit the ground hard and grazed her left arm. She took a look over her shoulder and spotted a figure heading towards her. It jolted her to her feet and she sprinted away. Though her arm was in some pain she was glad she hadn't twisted her ankle in the fall. Finally, after what seemed like an eternity she reached the tall trees. Celeste breathed heavily. She held one hand over her mouth and listened.

Nothing.

Celeste had to look. Pressed against the tree she slowly moved her body to face the resort. She couldn't see Rob anymore and there was no figure chasing her.

Calm down Celeste she told herself.

As she started to rotate even further around the tree Celeste was hit. She looked down and saw a flash of red as she crumbled to the ground. Celeste had the strength to pull the dart from her leg as she lay next to the tree. It read '*Tranquiliser*' on the side.

Celeste couldn't fight anymore and she felt herself fading away. As her eyes began to close a man stood over her and grinned.

It was a figure from her past.

Celeste blacked out.

7.

Lawsov and Wilkins both looked disbelievingly at Rob.

"So…it was a tranquilliser dart?" started Wilkins.

"Yes."

"Are you sure that's what it was?" asked Lawsov.

"Yes…I told you Celeste read the side of it."

Rob was beyond tired and he was sick of re-treading old ground.

"But *you* never read the side of it did you?"

This is bullshit. You're keystone cops and I can't believe this is taking so long.

"What? Isn't that believable?"

"Do you need to make this story 'believable'?" pressed Wilkins with a smarmy look.

"No, it's the truth!"

Rob rubbed his eyes. The lighting was dim and the fluorescent bulbs were starting to get to him.

"Listen Rob. It's my duty to tell you that you are a suspect in this case."

This flipped Rob from tired to angry.

"Hold on… Me? Why?"

"Call it circumstantial at this stage," Wilkins stated. "Wrong place wrong time."

"What does that even mean?"

"I just want you to help me get my facts straight Rob."

He tried to calm down. Rob didn't like being the centre of attention at a party much less the suspect of a murder investigation. His mouth was dry but he refused to ask for water.

"I'm here, telling you the truth and you…"

He was interrupted by Lawsov sniggering across the desk "yeah… truth."

"Look, the tranquiliser gun is a bit much."

"I still have bruising!" Rob said pointing two fingers at his neck. There was a dark bruise forming under the skin. Lawsov wasn't buying it and stared Rob in the eyes.

"Could be from anywhere… work… home…"

"What? Are you insinuating that I get *beaten* at home?"

"You said it, not me."

Lawsov knew if he pushed hard enough Rob would have to push back eventually. The cracks were starting to show. As the pressure built Wilkins offered an olive branch.

"He's not suggesting anything except that for all we know you could be the killer. We're paid to be sceptical."

Rob considered the facts. They could only hold him for so long without charging him and that time must be approaching. He hadn't asked for a lawyer yet and given that he was now a suspect that was looking like a good option right now.

"I told you what happened."

"And your story may be just that – a story. It's a version of events that seems rather convenient." Lawsov and Wilkins shared a look and Rob stood up in frustration. For the first time he was eye to eye with the detectives. He fought back tears as he looked from Lawsov to Wilkins.

"Have you been to the cave? Have you found the bodies?"

Bodies. Rob couldn't believe how much things had changed.

"Look, we'll get to that. For now can you keep telling us *the truth*?"

Wilkins motioned to the chair hoping Rob would take his place. He wanted the truth and maybe the best way to get it was to let Rob dig his own grave. He watched him slump back into the chair with a reluctant sigh.

"I got shot with a tranquilliser dart," he stated calmly.

"Okay, then what happened?"

8.

It must have been a long time before Rob woke up. He was sore and disorientated from the tranquiliser so he didn't immediately recognise his surroundings. Rob found himself lying on his side against a metal grill that had left indents across his arms. He stretched as much as he could but found he was trapped inside a steel cage. He turned to find Celeste lying beside him. Rob had passed out in front of her and it was strange to see her here now.

What's going on? Where the hell are we?

She was unusually still and her face looked quietly into the distance. Rob looked around and found that they were inside a cave. He didn't remember passing any caves on the way to the resort, which only added to his confusion. There was enough natural sunlight in the distance and Rob could see the tracks where the two of them had been dragged in. Upon closer inspection the cage looked homemade but as Rob tried to find a way out he realised it was impossible to break from the inside. He felt his neck where the dart had pierced his skin. It had come out of nowhere and he didn't remember a thing.

Who did this to us? Rob thought as he pulled himself off the ground.

"Celeste? What happened?"

Celeste spoke in a timid voice that Rob had never heard before.

"I'm scared Rob."

"Don't worry... we'll get out of here," he said without thinking. Rob noted that there were several lights set up and a few cardboard boxes in the open space with them. Nothing was within arms-reach though.

Does someone live here?

"Are you alright?" Celeste asked.

"Yeah... I feel like..." he stopped and decided it was best not to worry her further. He felt like he had been hit with a sledgehammer and then collapsed in an awkward position.

"Are *you* alright Celeste?"

"Yes," she lied.

What is Gordon going to do to us?

She hadn't seen his face in years yet here he was. Gordon Lewis.

Shit.

Celeste and Rob sat up and assessed their surroundings. Though Rob was genuinely afraid for their lives he tried to stay calm. He knew so little about this situation and seeing Celeste so panicked didn't help things. He called out towards the cave entrance.

"HELP!!!"

They took turns to no avail. Celeste pressed her mouth between the bars of the cage and screamed in frustration and fear.

"CAN ANYONE HEAR ME? HEEEEELP!"

"HEEEEEEELP"

Celeste closed her eyes and gave up. A figure stepped out from the darkness and spoke four words that sent a chill down Celeste's spine.

"I can hear you."

He has been here the whole time.

Rob immediately recognised Gordon and knew from the smug detached look on his face that he was almost certainly their captor. He stood about a metre from the cage and folded his arms. Gordon wore jeans and a plain grey shirt instead of the Resort uniform Rob had previously seen him in. His clothes had a layer of dirt on them and he seemed taller but it was probably the angle.

"You!" Rob proclaimed in a state of shock.

Gordon chuckled quickly.

"Yes. *Surprise,*" he said jokingly. This was no laughing matter and Rob could feel his skin turn red with agitation. He was right to be suspicious of Gordon's intentions. He had sensed something was off but he couldn't have imagined this.

"What the hell is going on here?"

Celeste remained still as Gordon crouched down to meet Rob's gaze.

"Well now I'm no genius, but it looks like you're stuck in a cage."

To emphasise the point Gordon rattled the bars shaking Celeste back to reality.

"Let us out now!" Rob shouted.

"Please?" smiled Gordon. He was in control and it was obvious he liked it.

I'm the alpha male now Rob.

"Let us out... please."

"Please...Gordon."

"What?"

"My name is Gordon"

Rob looked at Gordon for a moment. He was almost within reach and Rob considered his options.

"Let us out *Gordon*" he said.

"You didn't say please..."

"Please" Celeste begged.

She couldn't look either man in the eye. Gordon looked longingly at Celeste, willing her to meet his gaze. She silently refused.

"Not a chance."

Rob grabbed the cage bars with both hands and screamed, "Goddamn it!"

Celeste's words had set something off in Gordon and he seemed less level headed than before. Rob thought about their conversation on the bridge.

"Goddamn *you!*" Gordon said looking directly at Rob "Damn you to hell for what you've done."

"What? You don't even know me."

"I know your type. And I sure as hell know hers."

Rob remembered Celeste talking about an ex-boyfriend named Gordon and knew this was no coincidence. He struggled to recall any details she may have mentioned about him and silently cursed his listening skills.

"Leave her out of this. What do you want? Money? If that's it then you've kidnapped the wrong guy. I can barely support myself."

This wasn't entirely true but Rob spoke so convincingly that Gordon believed him.

"Does she know that?"

"Please just let me go," whispered Celeste.

"Does she know *what?*"

"Does she know you have no money? It's a simple question."

The Trent report was the furthest thing from his mind now. Rob figured there would be no negotiating with Gordon.

"You're not after my money are you?"

"No."

You want Celeste.

Gordon stood up and started pacing. He was calm and collected again.

"This isn't about money or fame or religion or power or because I'm some psychopath."

Rob cringed at the word 'psychopath' and Gordon took notice.

"Hey, if I wanted revenge or sex I'd have taken it by now."

Gordon caught Celeste looking and though he spun to face her as quickly as he could she looked away.

"Well, that's not completely true."

"Then what *is* this about?"

"Do you want to guess?"

Rob had already guessed.

"Just tell me."

"It's about her."

It's always about her.

Rob looked at Celeste and his heart sank.

"How do you know him?" he asked, already knowing the answer.

Gordon couldn't help but interrupt "You're going to love this."

Celeste opened her mouth but couldn't speak.

"How do you know him?" Rob repeated. He felt sick with anticipation. Rob assumed they had dated, he was sure she hadn't been with *two* men named Gordon, but wanted to hear her confirm it. She was too quiet and it was bothering him.

Goddamn it Celeste. Say something.

"Tell him Celeste," goaded Gordon "he wants to know."

"He's my ex-boyfriend."

This was Gordon's moment. His plan was working and he was thrilled.

"Ex-fiancée! I often wonder why we didn't work out too. Why don't you tell him about *that* Celeste?"

"I don't want to."

"Then you don't have to," said Rob as he did his best to show Celeste he was still on her side.

What the fuck Celeste.

"Oh! Why not?" asked Gordon.

"It's in the past."

Rob wished Gordon had stayed in the past too.

Had Celeste known he would be here? Had he been led into a trap? Rob suddenly imagined the two of them together, in cahoots. He had a horrible sensation in the pit of his stomach that they were conning him. Maybe that was why Celeste hadn't had sex with him.

Is she still in love with Gordon?

Gordon continued, "We've all got a past. Hers got you both here. You sure you don't want to know?"

Gordon was dying to tell Rob. He had butterflies swimming inside him. Neither of them knew how long he had waited for this moment. Gordon fantasised about Celeste walking past him on the street. He saw her face in his dreams. He missed everything they used to be. Gordon needed her. Rob was determined not to give away his true feelings.

"I want you to. I really do." Gordon turned to face Celeste and changed to a more sinister tone "besides, it will be good for Rob to know what lies ahead. What kind of *woman* you are."

It was clear that Gordon was harbouring some intense feelings. The light from the cave entrance had dimmed and Rob assumed the menacing clouds had arrived.

"Tell him the story Celeste," commanded Gordon.

"Why? What will that solve?" she pleaded.

"Tell it now or else I will shoot Rob with more than just a tranquiliser dart."

Gordon reached his arm back and pulled a small 9mm handgun from his belt. Her eyes went wide.

SHIT.

Rob tried to charge the side of the cage but couldn't get enough of a run up to cause it any trouble. Gordon slowly removed a silencer and started screwing it into the barrel of the gun. He cocked his head to the side and waited for Celeste to start talking.

He's going to shoot him.

"Stop... please."

"This is really going to hurt," Gordon said as he pointed the gun casually at Rob.

"I'll tell him... just... please." Celeste tried to compose herself as tears started to escape from her eyes. Gordon lowered his gun.

"I'm waiting."

The intensity of the situation was too much and Celeste began to break down.

"This is going to be hard to hear," she said between sobs.

9.

Celeste and Gordon had been going out for just over a year when their friends Helena and Tony got pregnant and decided to have a big party before the baby came. Their house had been transformed into a tropical paradise and Gordon had already taken advantage of the unattended bar. They were his friends but she was happy to be invited. Celeste was sober and ready to go home. Gordon took a swig of his drink and grinned.

"Are you having fun honey?" she asked.

"Yeah this is great!" he replied. The alcohol had taken over and Gordon was like a pig in mud.

"I hope this might make up for not seeing me all week?"

Gordon was sympathetic and rubbed Celeste's leg. "I know you've gotta work..." he said. Celeste had paintings to finish for her gallery opening. She couldn't control herself and had to paint. She was inspired.

"It's going to be a great party!" said Gordon.

"I'm sorry I have to go... I really wish I could stay."

"I understand."

Celeste's passion was painting and even though it was dragging her away from him Gordon could tell it made her happy.

"I love you," Celeste said.

"I love you more," Gordon countered.

To anyone outside the relationship they seemed happy. Celeste wasn't so sure about Gordon. Gordon was determined to have a good time and celebrate Helena and Tony's impending bundle of joy. He kissed Celeste goodnight and headed over to the bar for another sneaky drink. He wondered about whether Celeste would want to have a baby soon. Celeste lingered at the window.

What have I done?

Out of the corner of his eye he spotted a figure lurking in the crowd. He squinted through the influence of the rum and saw sharp green eyes and flowing brown hair. A girl was staring at him and smiling. Gordon smiled back and returned to his drink. Each time Gordon looked in her direction she had moved closer and each time her eyes remained locked on him. This wasn't out of the ordinary for Gordon. He had spent his youth being objectified by women and he loved the attention. She stood beside him and leaned into the makeshift bar. Gordon could see she was absolutely stunning and had to engage her. The rum had given him unlimited confidence without any thought for consequences.

"I'm Gordon."

"I know."

She shook his outstretched hand and held it for much longer than was socially acceptable.

"I'm Gwen."

Gordon smirked as he watched Celeste deteriorate before his eyes. It was satisfying to feel in control of things again. He had started to get answers.

The truth.

"Ah yes, it's all coming back to me. We were happy. We were engaged."

Celeste quickly chimed in with "I wasn't happy." She was putting on a show for Rob but she was trying to convince herself as well.

"Yes you were. You were happy until that night."

Rob felt sick but he had to know.

"What happened?" he asked.

Gordon thought back to that night with Gwen. Things had escalated when Gwen's feet started to hurt. They were new shoes and the excuse of removing them had led Gwen and Gordon to a secluded room. Gordon hadn't planned it but when they were alone it was as if a chemical reaction had ignited the air in the room. Gwen had sat tantalisingly close to Gordon and there was a real art to the way she pouted that made him want to kiss her. Gwen had been so accessible somehow while also being a complete mystery. In that moment he hadn't even considered Celeste. Gordon leaned closer without thinking and Gwen slid her hand onto his cheek. She angled her head slightly, inviting Gordon to kiss her.

He felt he had no other choice and thrust himself at her. It was primal. They shared a long and tender kiss that ended only because Gordon had been holding his breath. Gwen had silently started to undo her dress by lowering the zipper at the side to reveal her breasts. She stepped up and let her dress fall to the floor. Gordon remained still. Gwen stepped towards him and lowered herself onto his lap. She put her arms around Gordon's neck and watched him stare helplessly at her chest. Someone from the party yelled something and for a moment Gordon realised what was happening. Gwen waited patiently for Gordon to react and after a time he moved his hands to her hips. She could feel his erection growing and she playfully started to move against it. Gordon thought about Celeste as he started kissing Gwen's lips.

This is happening.

10

"You cheated on me with Gwen."

Celeste had not made eye contact with either Rob or Gordon for a while and now stared at the cave floor. It was the same shade of brown as her short shorts. Gordon tried his best to offer a sincere apology. He clasped his hands in front of him as he spoke as if he were begging for forgiveness. The barrel of the gun shone through his fingers.

"Yes I did. I'm sorry Celeste."

Maybe he just wants to apologise? That can't be it. Remember the tranquiliser darts.

"Look, this is all ancient history... please just let us go Gordon."

Celeste spoke in a small voice. Celeste kept her eyes fixed on the gun. It was much easier for her to watch the gun than to look at Rob. He was uncomfortable against the steel of the cage and kept shifting his body weight.

"Now Rob, when you hear that story I don't doubt that I look like a bad guy."

Rob stared at Gordon.

"Be honest I can take it."

It was clear that he would have to talk to Gordon if they were to have any hope of getting out of that cave alive.

Maybe we can negotiate ourselves out of here. Or maybe he will let me go and I can run for help.

"You still look like the bad guy," he said.

Gordon was defiant, "I'm not though," he returned, as he stood taller than ever.

"I couldn't be with you after that night" Celeste fired at Gordon.

Gordon knelt down in front of Celeste leaving her no choice but to look at him. He was very close to her face, daring her to reach out to him. He hadn't changed that much since they had dated. If anything he had lost weight and gained muscle.

"I know I lost your trust, but I think I could get it back."

Celeste was fuming.

"How? By threatening me? Or shooting Rob? By bringing us... here?"

Why did she put the idea of shooting ME in his head? Rob wondered.

Gordon looked around the cave. To him it had become like a second home.

"Do you like it here? It's a little place I used to come to think about us."

"There *is* no us."

Gordon reached out to touch Celeste through the bars of the cage but stopped himself.

"You know the first time I came up here I was lost. It was pouring… and I came in out of the rain… just kind of found this cave in the hillside. It's really something I think. I wound up sleeping here. Right over there."

Gordon looked nostalgically over to a flat area of the cave.

He's like a caveman. He clubbed Celeste over the head and dragged her back to his cave like a Neanderthal.

Rob didn't want to die. He imagined a news reporter standing outside the cave as paramedics wheeled out their bodies in the background. He thought about how they would flash up his Facebook profile picture, or one of the two of them together. He tried to think of a headline.

JILTED LOVER MURDERS EX AND PARTNER.

He would be a footnote in the story. It was all about Celeste even in death.

'She must have been worth killing for,' would be the water cooler conversation.

"Let us go" Rob pleaded.

LOVE TRIANGLE ENDS IN TRAGEDY.

"I can't do that."

"Why are you doing this?" Celeste asked, afraid of the answer.

Gordon might just need closure.

"You set me up."

"No I didn't."

"She told Gwen to seduce me because she wanted to see if I would go for it."

Celeste pulled a face that confirmed her complete surprise. She had no idea that Gordon had figured that out.

"I was right wasn't I? I was right about you," she said.

"I'm only human Celeste. You're not perfect either."

He's going to kill us. Slowly.

Rob sat silently trying to process the situation.

Celeste set him up? She sent another woman, this Gwen, to seduce Gordon?

Rob thought hard and tried to deduce whether any of the women he had met in the last nine months could have been Gwen. There were few women that talked to Rob, mostly his co-workers. Would she have tried this with him? She was engaged to Gordon and they were only dating.

"What can I do about any of this now?" Celeste asked.

"You didn't want to face me. Didn't want to follow through with your little game."

"I didn't really feel like talking to you."

"You weren't even brave enough to tell me it was over. You left and I had to hear it all from Gwen," Gordon said as his nostrils flared and he turned his attention to Rob.

"Now, what I want to know from you *Rob* is this…" he said as he passed the gun from one hand to the other, "how long have you two been going at it?"

"You've got nothing to do with us," Rob said as he tried to maintain a united front. It was becoming difficult.

Gwen. The name rolled around in his head.

"I just want to know if she was seeing you when she was seeing me. If she used Gwen as an easy way out… Maybe she wasn't happy. Don't you wanna know Rob? If she's the hypocrite I think she is?"

Rob did want to know. Sometimes *he* wanted an easy way out. Confrontation wasn't his strong suit and he knew deep down that if he ever really wanted to break up with Celeste that he wouldn't know where to begin. If Gwen showed up and she was as attractive as he imagined she must be then he knew in his heart he would probably cheat on Celeste. He hated himself for thinking it but it was the truth.

"No" he stated unconvincingly.

"You trust her then?"

"Of course" Rob lied.

THREE DEAD IN CAVE MOUNTAIN MURDER SUICIDE.

Gordon could see that Rob was scared to know the truth.

"I trusted her too. That was before though. Maybe she's changed huh? Maybe people change... but that's not how the saying goes. I don't trust her. I have absolutely no reason not to trust *you* yet... I know you and I are both just looking for the truth. Can I trust you Rob?"

"I'm not like you."

Rob believed it too.

Celeste hadn't known Gordon worked here. She didn't want to ever see him again.

"You're not like *me*?" Gordon pressed. "Not yet. But you've been blind to it. I'm just trying to help you see."

Celeste and Rob accidently looked up at the same time and locked eyes. Celeste's eyes had filled with fear and regret. Her breathing had slowed and she had become an entirely different person in this extreme situation. Rob could see that each time she responded it was to mask the fear that they might not get out of here alive.

"You think she loves you more than she loved me?" Gordon was never going to stop until he got an answer. Rob would have to speak for them both.

"Nine months."

Gordon was taken aback with the abrupt answer.

"Nine months?" he repeated.

"Yes."

"She left me about ten months ago."

Rob was somewhat relieved.

"I never cheated on either of you," a vindicated Celeste spoke up defiantly.

"But… I was your rebound guy?" Rob whispered to Celeste.

The cracks got wider.

"No…it's not like…"

"It's not like you were engaged?" asked Rob.

He had chosen not to focus on the engagement initially but it was a thorn in his side.

Why hasn't she told me about any of this? Why didn't I know she was engaged to this asshole?

Celeste trailed off. She was losing Rob's support and it made her feel terrible.

"You know what I think?" Gordon interjected "I think she doesn't love you Rob. She only loves herself."

"Gordon..." Celeste started to speak but she couldn't find the rest of the sentence.

"Think about it" he smiled back "I'll see you tomorrow."

"Don't leave us," Celeste managed.

"I'm sorry I have to go... I *really* wish I could stay," he said mockingly. It was the exact wording Celeste had used when she left the party that night. Gordon doubted that the reference would mean anything to her now but it felt good to say it. He didn't turn around as he walked out of the cave into the evening air. It was fresh and Gordon felt like a new man.

There was an eerie silence in the cave as Rob listened to Gordon's footsteps fade away. The ink on Rob's fingers had dried and now served as a reminder of a time before Gordon had entered their lives.

"Why didn't you tell me about any of this?" he asked Celeste.

"What could I say?"

She's answering my question with a question.

"Maybe mentioning you were engaged a month before you met me?"

Secrets and lies. What else isn't she telling me?

"It wasn't important."

"It *was* important" Rob grunted in disgust "obviously."

Celeste could feel every inch of space between them as she spoke.

"I didn't think you wanted to know about my past. It had nothing to do with us."

"Well, it's affecting us now isn't it?"

"I'm sorry Rob." Celeste didn't know what to say. Rob was here because of her. They were trapped because of her. The holiday was a disaster and everything was her fault.

"I…I can't talk to you right now" Rob said as he shifted away again.

"Maybe I deserve that," she said, words filled with sorrow.

You absolutely DO deserve that. You deserve worse.

She was hoping Rob would keep talking but he didn't. It became darker as they lay down in the cave. Rob had resigned himself to the fact that they would be spending the night there and he was determined to do so in silence.

If Gordon can sleep here how bad can it be?

Rob was furiously planning a way to get them both out alive so that he could be rid of her once and for all.

He wanted Celeste to live a long life knowing that he hated her and always would.

Fuck you Celeste.

In a nearby shed Gordon washed his hands in a bucket of soapy water. He stood looking at his reflection in the mirror and thought about what tomorrow would bring. Gordon took a black electric shaver and began shaving his head.

I'm going to get Celeste back he thought as he shortened his hair. It looked like a military haircut.

Perfect.

He focused on a picture of himself with Celeste. It had been taken in the days following their engagement. Celeste wore a tight fitting floral shirt and had her hair up in a bun. Gordon wore a blue shirt eerily similar to the one Rob wore now. He was kissing Celeste on the cheek but they were both looking at the camera when the photo was taken. They seemed to look through the picture at Gordon now. This image of how his life should have been was beckoning him.

She belongs with me.

Gordon smiled and brushed fallen hair from his bare shoulders. He couldn't wait for tomorrow.

11

Rob burst out of the water and took a gulp of air. He used to swim on his lunch breaks and had always enjoyed the repetitive exercise. He wondered why he ever stopped going. One of the few advantages to being the only people staying at the resort was that the indoor pool was completely empty. It was a fairly big room with frosted windows all around the pool area. Rob was feeling refreshed and floated on his back with his ears submerged under the waterline. As he looked up at the ceiling he heard someone coming in and spun around to see Celeste standing poolside. She wore a pink two- piece swimsuit and had a white towel over her shoulder and one in her hand.

"You forgot your towel," she said smiling.

"Thanks."

She looks fantastic.

Placing the towels nearby she pulled her hair up in a ponytail and dived into the pool. "It's nice isn't it?" he asked as she surfaced.

"Yeah," she replied and splashed him in the face.

"Hey!"

"Hey yourself!" she laughed, "Why didn't you wait for me?"

"You were taking ages" Rob rolled his eyes, "as usual."

"That's because it's a new swimsuit. Did you notice?"

"Yeah now that you mention it…"

It looks expensive.

"Do you…*like it?*"

The pink top was padded and gave the illusion of ample breasts. Celeste subtly leaned forward to draw Rob's eye.

"I do. I like it."

"I got it for the beach but since we're here now I thought I would bring it."

"You brought it alright."

Celeste smiled at the compliment. She swam into Rob's arms and gave him a kiss.

"Thanks again for coming," she said as she kissed him.

"I love you Celeste."

"I love you too."

It was a perfect moment. Rob ran his hands up Celeste's arms. She had tan lines from the sleeves of her t-shirt.

"Sorry about forgetting the anniversary," he said earnestly.

"You can make it up to me when we get to a year!" she said as she gave him a hug.

"Well that's good!" he said "I'm glad we're going to *make* it to a year."

"Of course we will," Celeste beamed "we love each other."

Celeste wrapped her legs around Rob's waist. The weightlessness of the water made it easy for her to float there with him. Rob pulled Celeste in for another kiss and held her close. She smiled and dipped her hand under the water and into Rob's shorts. She had Rob literally in the palm of her hand. They hadn't had sex in a while and they had never had sex anywhere in public. The frosted windows gave Celeste confidence and she stopped to remove her top. Rob's jaw hit the bottom of the pool.

"What are you doing?" he asked.

"C'mon Rob. Kiss me."

He didn't need to be told twice. Celeste and Rob had hurried adolescent sex in the swimming pool. It was like they were starting their relationship again. Celeste gave him a tender kiss when they were done. Rob was content. He looked at her and watched her face change. She suddenly went from beautiful and angelic to vacant and distant. Celeste wrapped her fingers around Rob's throat and pushed him under the water. Rob thrashed and kicked but couldn't stop her. Celeste seemed to have stolen his strength from him. His lungs filled with water and his vision blurred. He saw a flash of pink swimmers as he struggled for his life. Rob woke in a cold sweat next to Celeste. The nightmare wasn't over.

12.

The door opened and a freshly shaved Gordon threw Thomas onto the floor of the living room. Thomas was almost seventy and knocking him down was an easy task for Gordon. Thomas, the owner of Lake Cook resort, had serious internal injuries.

"For God's sake Gordon," Thomas said as he clutched his side in pain.

"God can't save you," said Gordon in a booming voice, "you must save yourself."

He was an atheist. If Gordon believed in God he would never have kidnapped Rob and Celeste.

Gordon had just cut the main phone lines so when Thomas picked up the Resort phone on the small side table he didn't flinch. Thomas's face dropped when he heard nothing on the other end.

"Why are you doing this?"

"You know why," Gordon responded as he stroked his head. He cut an imposing figure above Thomas. The effect was magnified by the angle at which Thomas cowered at his feet. Thomas coughed and felt blood in his throat.

"Celeste?" he managed to ask.

"Of course."

"I know it's hard now that she's here but you must accept that she's moved on."

Thomas's face did nothing to mask the pain of his injuries and he clutched his abdomen. Gordon bent down low and gave him another shove as he spoke.

"She still has my ring on her finger."

She must want to be with me.

"Okay, so even if she hasn't moved on, what can you say? It's up to her."

"I don't need to *say* anything. I don't need to win her over with words. I'm getting rid of the boyfriend - and you - and when we are alone at last I can just keep Celeste here."

The words sounded insane as Gordon said them. Thomas tried to speak clearly and calmly.

"That's not going to work..."

"I don't *care!*

Gordon was acting like a petulant child. Thomas managed to kneel which lessened the pain in his mid section.

He's lost his mind. How can I reason with him?

"She won't be happy Gordon. You can't force someone to love you."

"Yes she will," Gordon said with a sadistic look in his eyes, "I'll keep her here until she remembers why she loved me."

"Why she loved you? Tell me Gordon. Why *did* Celeste love you?"

Gordon faced away from Thomas and stood almost completely still. There was no easy answer for Gordon. He was sure he had loved Celeste and she had loved him. There wasn't a *reason* for it. In that moment Gordon decided that he would do anything for Celeste. That was love.

"I pity you," said Thomas.

Gordon spun around on the spot.

"You don't pity me, I pity *you*."

"Beating up a blind man makes you feel special does it? Get it over with would you?"

"I'm not going to kill you," stated Gordon "unless you get in my way."

"You're not thinking clearly mate."

"I am *mate*. Celeste is my girl. It's time I got her back."

"Gordon, I'm hurt."

"You'll be fine. It's nothing personal. You'll probably thank me for this."

"Thank you for *what*?"

Gordon walked straight up to Thomas and took him by the throat. A painting of a naval ship captain stared down at Gordon as he picked Thomas up and slammed him through the coffee table. A combination of glass and wood shattered upon impact. Thomas groaned in agony and Gordon's eyes went wide in surprise. He hadn't intended to do so much damage but was giddy with the results. There was adrenaline pumping through Gordon.

I don't know my own strength he thought as he looked at the pieces scattered from one wall to another.

Gordon couldn't see that a large piece of glass had pierced Thomas's side. He had started bleeding into the light brown carpet. Gordon paid him no attention as he scooped up a piece of wood on his way to the door.

A memento.

"Gordon! Gordon wait!" pleaded Thomas. He was dying and the shock of his landing had made him incoherent.

Gordon glanced back from the doorway.

"You'll stay out of my way Thomas if you know what's good for you. Celeste is *meant* to be with me."

It would be the last thing Thomas would ever hear.

13.

Neither of them slept particularly well against the base of the cage. Rob spent most of the night silently internalising his growing hatred while Celeste tried to somehow pry her way out. She was thin but she wasn't quite thin enough to squeeze through the bars. The night had left them exhausted. They were both nearing breaking point when Rob heard footsteps and sat up. Gordon headed into the cave with several black garbage bags in hand. Rob couldn't help but see the headline.

BODY PARTS FOUND IN GARBAGE BAGS.

Gordon dropped them all near the entrance except one. Strutting towards them he soaked up each moment as he spoke.

"Rob - thanks for not unpacking. It made it much easier to check you both out of the resort..." he turned on the spot "and into the cave. I'd like to welcome you both."

Celeste did not speak. Rob had been gripping the bars of the cage in front of him.

"Are you enjoying your stay?" Gordon joked. He was suitably dressed in the Lake Cook resort shirt again. At this moment Rob noticed Gordon's shaved head. It was a sinister look that made Gordon seem far more evil. Gordon noticed him looking.

"How are you doing Rob?"

"Like you care."

"If you need to go to the bathroom maybe Celeste and I can turn around? Make you feel more comfortable?"

This comment threw Rob and he fell back into negotiations with Gordon.

"Look… let us go now. We won't press charges… We'll just leave, okay?"

"No."

"Let me go then. You want Celeste? Let *me* go." Rob wondered if this tactic would work. He felt Celeste shoot him a look and assumed it was disappointment. Gordon wasn't biting and ignored Rob.

He put his hand in the black garbage bag and pulled out some lingerie. They were red and black and belonged to Celeste.

"I remember these. Have you seen these Rob?" Gordon enquired. Rob had seen them a few times early in their relationship but this was their first appearance in months. Rob remembered a carefree time before the resort, before the Trent report and even before Celeste. Had he been happy for the last nine months with Celeste? He had to stay on track and find a way to escape.

"What are we in here for? Are you going to kill us?" he asked.

What the hell do you want? Rob thought.

Gordon continued to ignore Rob. He was here to deal with Celeste. Rob was to be tolerated – for now. He chuckled in sadistic enjoyment for a moment before continuing.

"Celeste, seeing you again... well... it's brought back a lot of memories."

That's an understatement.

Rob scanned Gordon's torso for a weapon but couldn't see the gun. He eyed the black bags suspiciously and listened as Gordon continued his speech.

"I want you to forgive me for Gwen. I'm sorry."

"Gordon, I... forgive you" Celeste said quietly.

Is she serious, Rob pondered, or is she trying to get out of here? Remember, she is better at deception than you've given her credit for.

"I want you back."

"What?" Rob couldn't contain himself.

Stay calm.

"Cel honey," spoke Gordon as he tried to get her attention, "I've missed you."

Celeste sat up and tried unsuccessfully to wipe the dirt from her face. Tears had been forming throughout the night and they were threatening to descend her cheeks.

"Listen to me Gordon, please. You must have known this wouldn't work. I mean I haven't spoken to you since I left, you haven't tried to call…"

"That's not true," interrupted Gordon "I called… I left messages! You cut me off."

Celeste remembered changing her phone number. Of course he tried to call.

"Gordon… things have changed since then."

Celeste forced her hand into Robs and held on tight.

"I'm with Rob now," she said.

Looks like she's taking me down with her.

It was an impossible scenario. Celeste wouldn't get back together with Gordon and he wouldn't set them free until she did. They were at an impasse. Gordon stood and kicked dirt at the happy couple. Celeste cringed and coughed in reaction to the attack, which made Gordon immediately sorry.

Stubborn bitch.

"So you're saying our engagement, our relationship was meaningless?" asked Gordon trying to make sense of it all.

"No, no…I'm not saying that. But our relationship has ended."

"And you're with him?"

"Yes. I'm with Rob."

Rob looked up to find Gordon sizing him up. He looked so much more intense with a shaved head.

"Then I'll get rid of him… and you'll be single again," Gordon said decisively.

"No!" screamed Celeste.

There it is.

It was the first implication of murder and it struck a chilling nerve with her. Celeste didn't want to be responsible for Rob's death.

How do we get out of this alive?

"Why should he have you if I can't? Why should *he* be happy? Tell me that!" Gordon shouted. He got down low and pressed himself against the cage forcing Celeste backwards.

"You never gave me back the ring… we're still engaged, it's like a contract."

Rob looked at the ring on Celeste's hand. She had worn that ring every day for the last nine months. Celeste had held on to a piece of this man. Gordon had been a presence every day of their relationship. Celeste wore the ring on her right hand but the sentiment remained.

"It was a gift," said Celeste, finally finding her voice. She looked to Rob.

"That ring?" asked Rob desperately.

"This was my engagement ring," Celeste nodded.

"You never told me."

"No."

"This is unbelievable," stammered Rob.

It's like I don't know you at all.

"You never took it off?" asked Gordon.

"No."

Gordon could feel Rob losing his grip on Celeste.

It's working. Celeste can't be alone. If Rob doesn't want her then she will have to be with me.

Rob's mind raced and he felt as though he was floating over his own body, watching the conversation unfold from afar.

"Why didn't you tell me about this? Is this another one of your games? Do you still love him?"

"Now we're getting somewhere." Gordon loved watching the fabric that bound them unravel.

"Shut the hell up!" said Rob as he rattled the cage.

"No, *you* shut up! Answer the question Celeste."

"You're finished when I get out. I'm through with this," seethed Rob.

I'm in charge here Rob.

"You're through? Yeah. You're through with Celeste, through *breathing* if that's what I want! What makes you think you'll EVER get out of there?"

Gordon took the gun from the back of his belt and aimed it at Rob.

His arm was straightened, and he clearly meant business. Celeste tried to talk him down. She gripped the thick cage bar that went horizontally around them and knew without a shadow of doubt that Gordon was capable of murder.

"Gordon, please…talk to me."

Her voice was like his kryptonite. Celeste's gambit had worked and Gordon could see that killing Rob now was the wrong move. If he wanted her back he had to be patient. Lowering his gun Gordon fired words at Rob instead.

"She loves me. You're the rebound guy."

"I want you to let me go," stated Celeste.

He's softening. There's still hope.

"I can't yet… I'll be back in a little while, I just need to take care of something… and then we'll be together."

Gordon was under the delusion that he and Celeste were getting back together. She decided to let him think that for now.

It might be my only chance of escaping this.

Celeste felt guilty for not considering Rob. Was she being selfish? All Rob had done was love her enough to take her on this trip and she was already thinking about abandoning him. Maybe she didn't really love him as much as she thought she did.

"I want to say something," said Gordon as he tucked the gun away "I haven't been too well without you Cel. I came up here a couple of months ago to escape."

"I know it's hard..." Celeste started, but Gordon waved his arm to stop her.

"Let me finish. It's taken me a long time to get to where I am now. I tried to get over you..."

Gordon put one hand over his mouth as if he was trying to hold the words inside.

"I want to be honest. I can't live without you. I've *always* loved you."

Gordon paused in anticipation.

Say you love me too.

Celeste couldn't lead him on. She had conned Gordon once before and now they were his prisoners. What would happen if he caught her in a lie again? She didn't trust that she could pretend to love him. She didn't love Gordon. If this were the real world she would have run to the police and taken out a restraining order against him. If she was going to escape at all it had to be *with* Rob. Gordon was the past and Celeste hoped Rob would be the future. She took a chance and sided with her heart. It felt like the right thing to do and she hoped she wouldn't regret it.

"I'm here with Rob," she said proudly. The move took Rob by surprise. The idea that Celeste was choosing him over Gordon made his hatred subside. He was still unsure they could move past the lies but he did appreciate the effort.

She loves me.

Gordon's face fell. He had laid his cards on the table and lost. He was out of ideas.

"You may have arrived with Rob but you'll leave with me. You came to me this time!" seethed Gordon.

"She's here with me Gordon," said Rob, surprising himself with the outburst.

Gordon ignored him.

"There's a reason you're here Celeste," he said as he walked out of the cave and into the rain. The clouds had turned dark.

There was a storm coming.

14.

The woman plunged her walking stick into the dirt. She brushed her hair out of her eyes and looked over to her companion. He had been leading the way and didn't want to admit that he might be lost, but she knew they had passed this way before. It looked like it could rain at any minute and she looked into the distance for shelter. She squinted and noticed a figure up ahead. It was a man with a gun in his hand.

"Get down!" she said and instinctively grabbed her friend. The two of them ducked down low to the ground and peered at him. He looked intense as he walked purposefully through the grass.

Who the hell was that?

"He must have come from those caves over there," she said quietly.

The caves were partially obscured by trees but it was the only place the man could have come from. They knew that even though it was certainly dangerous, they had to find out if there was anyone else in that cave. They waited until he was almost out of their sight and then crept forward not knowing what they might find. A clap of thunder announced the arrival of rain and both hikers pressed towards the cave. The dirt was now turning to mud.

Inside the cage Celeste lay on her back and felt like she was floating. Her stomach turned and she realised how long it had been since they had eaten. The satay chicken dinner seemed like weeks ago. She had let herself fall in love with Gordon and it had been a terrible mistake. If she and Rob got out of this cage alive would they stay together? Celeste hadn't been alone in a long time and was often defined by the person she was with. She could see that Rob was utterly destroyed emotionally. She had never seen him look so deflated. This was a stress that their relationship had never endured before and Celeste became convinced that this was the end. Rob saw her looking and broke the silence.

"How did it get this far?"

"Gordon is a psycho…" Celeste started.

"…I meant us."

"Us?" Celeste wasn't sure what to say.

"You still love Gordon," Rob concluded aloud. He was sick and tired of the games and decided that even though this wasn't the place for a confrontation it would have to be the time for one.

"No I don't," she replied. It wasn't as convincing as Rob would have liked.

Let's just get this all out in the open.

"How can that be true? You still wear the ring."

The evidence was right there on Celeste's finger. Rob's mild mannered façade had faded away. Her eyes darted around as she tried to explain.

"It's not like that… it was a gift."

"And you *do* love him!" shouted Rob.

Celeste shoved Rob into the cage as best she could from a seated position.

"I said *NO*."

"Yes you do...you're lying."

Rob thought about choking Celeste at that moment. She had brought him to Lake Cook resort and now they were going to die. If Gordon came back and saw Celeste was dead he would just shoot Rob and this would all be over.

Enough is enough.

"I can't believe this. Why do I keep picking these kinds of guys?" Celeste said as she started to cry. The rain outside the cave was getting heavier.

"What's that supposed to mean?" asked Rob. He didn't like being compared to Gordon.

Celeste thought about their time together and ruined the last of her mascara wiping away tears. Rob had been the exact *opposite* of Gordon. She might have rebounded a little at the beginning of their relationship but it had grown into something she couldn't live without. Knowing that she could lose Rob had made Celeste realise how much she still needed him.

"Rob, I'm still in love with you."

He refused to speak.

"I love you Rob."

I'm trapped.

"After all this? You can't expect me to believe that," Rob scoffed. He was slightly ashamed that he had considered murdering her a moment ago.

"It's true."

Bullshit.

Rob fell silent. There was no point fighting anymore. Rob didn't have any fight left. It felt so familiar. Celeste held hands with him and he decided to let her. For the first time in a long time he had the upper hand. He wasn't worried that she would leave him. He wasn't worried about the Trent report or about getting a pay rise. He was worried about staying alive and whether or not this relationship was worth saving.

"You work too much and I know about your smoking... I don't care about that by the way."

"You knew about that?" Rob was taken aback. He thought he had been so stealthy, but James Bond he was not.

"Yeah, you shouldn't need to hide things from me Rob."

What hypocrisy that was.

"You're one to talk!" he shot back.

Deceiving each other had become the norm and it was time to come clean. Nothing else was working.

Honesty is the best policy.

"I made a mistake. I don't know what to say," said Celeste. She could feel the tears welling again.

Rob hated it when Celeste was upset. Once when she had been watching a sad movie he felt so terrible that he cleaned the bathroom. In retrospect he wondered why he didn't just comfort her.

"Say anything!"

"I'm sorry! I'm sorry! I don't know how many times I can say it…"

He watched as she fell apart in front of him. She had gotten through to him and Rob no longer had murderous thoughts on the mind.

"You need to be honest with me, okay?"

"I know that. I love you and I don't want anyone else."

"Not even Gordon?"

"I'd rather die than date him again," she said with hatred in her voice.

"That's not funny. He's not stable," said Rob. "We *could* die here."

They were back on the same side again, at least for now. Celeste tried to stop crying as she went on.

"We may not be alive tomorrow… I need you to know how I feel… just in case. And I'm so sorry for bringing you into this." Celeste meant it too. Her original plan of a romantic getaway had been anything but.

"I never meant to hurt you."

"Celeste..."

Rob and Celeste stared at each other. They were trapped and the situation was dire.

"It's not your fault," Rob said softly as he wiped away a tear from Celeste's cheek.

"Yes it is..."

"This is stupid," he said. "I love you."

Celeste melted when he said those words. In a mix of fear and emotion she threw herself into Rob and they kissed. In was extremely uncomfortable within the confines of the cage, but it was such a breakthrough moment that neither seemed to mind. Rob held onto Celeste and finally allowed himself to cry. Though the circumstances weren't ideal somehow this trip was bringing them together after all. They continued to kiss as the rain eased. An unfamiliar voice from the cave entrance finally interrupted them.

"Are you two alright?"

A rugged male hiker strode towards them taking both Rob and Celeste by surprise. He shook the cage violently looking for a way to open it as his female companion leaned against the wall of the cave. They were both soaking wet and she was obviously more out of breath than he was. Rob realised he had seen these two before. They were the hikers that they had driven past on the way to the resort. Celeste was the first to react.

"Thank God."

Celeste wasn't particularly religious but under the circumstances Rob understood the sentiment.

"Are you alright? What's going on here?" the male hiker asked.

"Please help us! We're trapped!" Rob managed. A burst of hope had given Rob and Celeste a new lease on life.

"Hang on… I'll try," he replied as he wedged his walking stick into the cage door for leverage. The walking stick was metal and the angle looked promising.

"Please hurry!" said Rob. "He'll be back soon."

"Who?"

"Gordon. The guy who put us in here," replied Rob.

"We'll help you. Don't worry."

Both men struggled with the cage, straining with each effort. It was only Celeste that noticed Gordon creeping back into the cave. She saw his eyes widen at the intrusion and as he raised a large kitchen knife into view, Celeste screamed.

"LOOK OUT!"

Gordon plunged the knife into the female hiker's back with such force that it seemed like it would burst through her front. She started nodding involuntarily as her body went limp and she collapsed to the cave floor. Her eyes stayed open as her heart gave its final beat. Gordon was still. He had killed this person without thinking and now realised what he had done. It was at this moment that the male hiker turned his head and saw his companions lifeless face looking back at him. He dropped the walking stick and charged at Gordon.

"You son of a bitch!" he yelled fighting back tears.

The two rolled to the ground in a ball of formidable aggression. Gordon started choking his attacker around the throat but he broke free. On any other day they might have been evenly matched but the hiker was being fuelled by rage and had the upper hand.

Rob and Celeste started bashing the cage. It had started to give way and with the right pressure was ready to pop open. Rob thought about the dying insect on the car dashboard that had given up in the heat. His body suddenly realised that it was in the same struggle as that insect and his legs started kicking violently at the cage. He could not give up. Meanwhile the struggle continued outside the cage. Gordon had reached for his gun in an effort to end the fight but the hiker had knocked it from his hand. The two were now inches from the female hikers corpse, which had becoming a very confronting image. Gordon managed to land several punches to the man's nose, breaking it in the process. It started to bleed onto both men.

After several more kicks the force was finally enough to break the cage open and Rob squeezed out. He made a grab for Gordon's gun and took it before anyone could react.

"Leave him alone!" Rob shouted at the two men.

They saw him pointing the gun and stopped fighting. The male hiker began to cry and released Gordon from his grasp. His face was now covered in blood from his nose.

It's over.

"It's alright Rob. We've stopped," Gordon offered.

Celeste pulled herself out of the cage. It had scraped her arm on the way but she didn't care. She was free. Rob moved himself to stand with Celeste. They were both so grateful to be free but at what cost? This woman – the same woman Rob had tried not to check out by the side of the road – was dead. Rob took his eyes off Gordon for only a moment but it was enough. In his grief the male hiker had not been paying attention and Gordon pulled the knife from one hiker and stabbed it into the other. It landed awkwardly into his neck and spurts of blood began to colour the dirt below.

Oh my God.

He fell and landed next to his companion. Their fate was sealed the moment they entered the cave.

We didn't even know their names.

Gordon looked at Celeste and saw her disappointment and fear. The veil had been lifted and she now viewed Gordon as the pure monster he had become. Rob was still pointing the gun at Gordon but hadn't been able to pull the trigger.

"Are you going to shoot me?" Gordon asked.

Is this how it ends?

He imagined Rob shooting him, then Celeste seeing *Rob* as the monster.

If I can't have her then neither will you.

"Don't shoot him Rob," said Celeste.

Rob was conflicted but tried to maintain his composure. This was a defining moment. He wasn't sure he could kill another man. The pool of blood now surrounded Rob's boot. The knife remained lodged in the neck of their rescuer.

Don't do this.

Celeste placed her hand onto Rob's shoulder and tried to calm him down.

"Please."

Gordon wore the bloodstains of his victims like a badge of honour. He stared through Rob without blinking.

"Shoot me Rob."

15.

Photos of the dead hikers now dominated the interrogation room table. Neither of them had closed their eyes at the moment of their death. Rob took his time looking at the pictures now. He noticed the beginnings of grey hair in the man's hairline and the shade of lipstick that the woman had been wearing that day. It was such a surreal feeling to have seen these people die. Rob concluded that this was the reason he had to wait. They had been to the caves and found the bodies. There would have been collecting evidence and now he was their prime suspect.

Lawsov drew a cigarette from his pocket and offered it to Rob. He shook his head.

"I thought you said you smoked," said Wilkins.

The mind games continued as Lawsov started to smoke the cigarette and then stubbed it out in front of Rob.

What a waste.

"I quit," Rob responded.

With the smell of nicotine floating in the air Rob found himself craving that cigarette.

"I guess you country cops are still allowed to smoke indoors, huh? They banned indoor smoking in the city."

Lawsov smiled and tapped the photos on the desk.

"Can you tell us anything else about the hikers?"

"Not really, no."

"We found blood on your boots Rob."

They had taken his boots citing standard protocol. Apparently, people had hung themselves using their shoelaces in holding cells in the past.

"I know, I stepped in it while we were in the cave."

"If you confess now..." started Wilkins. He paused and assessed Rob's face.

Confess? To what - murder?

"There are no surveillance cameras at Lake Cook resort. We can only determine what happened up there by talking to the survivors."

What use are surveillance cameras to a blind man.

"I'm trying to help you. That's why I came here." Rob was doing his best to remain calm but the pictures on the desk were making him nervous.

"I know that. Look at this from my point of view. You and your girlfriend were fighting, so you were angry."

"I didn't kill anyone."

"Your fingerprints are on the gun," said Lawsov without looking up from his notes.

"So are Gordons!"

"I'm going to find out the truth," said Wilkins. "One way or another."

It sounded like a threat to Rob. He stood up and started leaning against the wall behind him. It felt good to stretch but he was still craving nicotine.

"What day did you check into the resort?" asked Lawsov.

"I told you this already," Rob said as he wiped his eyes, "Saturday."

Wilkins leaned back in his chair as he spoke.

"Well, it's the weirdest thing. Paul and Nicole reported a car accident by phone on Saturday afternoon."

Rob determined that Paul and Nicole must have been the names of the deceased hikers. He suddenly remembered the abandoned car on the way to Lake Cook resort. Had it belonged to the two hikers? He felt sick to his stomach. When they were in need by the side of the road Rob and Celeste had driven right past. The hikers had found them in the cave and saved them. They'd saved their lives. Rob couldn't help but think about the way he'd let them die. The photos on the desk only made him feel worse. Rob was glad he'd moved to the back of the room and didn't have to look into their dead eyes.

"Anything you want to talk about?" asked Wilkins.

"No."

"Well, weren't you arriving that way with your girl?" enquired Lawsov "Did you see them on Saturday?"

Rob shook his head but then nodded. It was enough to make him seem even more suspicious to the Constables.

"Wrong place, wrong time," Lawsov said to Wilkins.

"That has nothing to do with this. We drove past when they were there. Nothing more."

Rob felt his words fall on deaf ears.

"I'm waiting for a phone call from the team we sent to the resort," announced Wilkins.

"Are they going to find anything we should hear about from you?"

Just more bodies. More death.

16.

Rob's hand was starting to shake now. Gordon was certain Rob could be talked into pulling the trigger. Celeste cowered behind Rob willing him not to shoot. If her boyfriend killed her ex-boyfriend in front of her she couldn't see herself recovering. It might also be a difficult sell for her next boyfriend.

Please.

Gordon had decided not to look down at the bodies. That part was over and he would learn to live with his actions. Or was this the end for him?

"Are you going to shoot me?"

"If I have to," replied Rob as confidently as he could. "Come on Celeste."

Rob started edging his way to the cave entrance and Celeste obediently followed.

She couldn't see Rob's eyes from where she was standing, and it made her very uneasy. She kept looking at Gordon who in turn didn't take his eyes off Rob.

"You don't need to do this," offered Celeste.

"Oh Celeste my love… do you want to know what Rob really thinks of this holiday? And you?" spoke Gordon while still maintaining Rob's gaze.

"Listen to me Gordon…I *will* shoot you."

"When Rob went for that walk the other day…"

As Gordon started speaking Rob stepped forward with the gun. The quick movement startled Celeste and she gasped. Rob was tired of Gordon assuming he was still in charge.

I've got the gun now Gordon.

Celeste looked on nervously.

"Rob doesn't wanna be here, he hates the outdoors," stated Gordon.

Compared to the well of secrets that had been unearthed here it was the weakest one yet.

Gordon is just trying to keep us here. He wants me to shoot him.

"He came here to be with me," said Celeste. "Rob wants to be with me. That's more than I can say for you."

Rob wasn't sure that he wanted to be with Celeste anymore. He was absolutely certain he didn't want to stay in this cave, because Gordon would eventually drive him to pull the trigger. He tried to calm himself down as he spoke to Gordon.

"I'm not sure you're worth killing. You're scum! You bring us up here... taunt us... try and steal my girl from me?"

"She was my girl first."

"WELL SHE'S MY GIRL NOW!" shouted Rob.

It took everyone by surprise and they all fell silent as the words echoed around the cave. Rob realised he was standing in blood and stepped back with his girlfriend.

"Rob… please… let's just go," said Celeste quietly to Rob. It was time to move.

"Get down on the ground Gordon."

Gordon slowly kneeled down.

"Right down," ordered Rob, "hands behind your head."

Gordon reluctantly lay down and placed his hands behind his head one at a time.

"If you come after us I will shoot you," said Rob matter-of-factly.

"There's nowhere you can go that I won't find you Robert."

It's still a joke to him thought Rob *I have the goddamn gun and he's laughing at me.*

"I wouldn't regret killing you," Rob said as he spat on the cave floor near Gordon.

"I'm sure Celeste would forgive you," replied Gordon, as he looked straight at her. "She forgave me."

Technically he was comparing infidelity to murder. It might take more than an apology to come back from that. There was an intense stare emanating from Gordon. A grin crept across his face.

"Rob is a better man than you," Celeste said spitefully.

"Gwen was better than you too."

Celeste was hurt, but only for a moment. Rob took her hand and the two of them ran out of the cave and into the rain.

Free at last.

They had fled in a non-specific direction. It turned out through pure chance that the cave entrance faced Lake Cook resort so after a short run Rob and Celeste could see their destination.

"Is Gordon chasing us?" yelled Celeste as they passed the trees where Rob had been tranquilised the day before.

"I don't see him," he responded. "Just keep running!"

Celeste was almost out of breath and doubled over. Neither of them had been eating or drinking during their ordeal and it was catching up to them. Rob looked down at the gun in his hand and felt ashamed. He hadn't wanted to kill Gordon; he had only wanted to protect Celeste.

I'm not like Gordon. I'm not a murderer.

"We can't stay here," he said and Celeste knew he was right.

"Hold on a minute," she said as she removed the ring from her finger.

Gordon may have loved her once but now all Celeste could feel was disgust that she had ever loved him back.

The ring shone in the sunlight and for a moment Rob thought he could read the inscription on the inside. It looked like it said '*Always*' but he couldn't be sure.

Celeste drew back her arm and hurled the ring into the lake. They both watched as it tumbled through the air, into the water and disappeared. In a moment of unison Rob threw Gordon's gun high in the air. It landed in the ripples created by the ring, bobbed up for a moment, and fell beneath the surface. Rob knew he could never pull the trigger. He was glad he didn't want to. Gordon was dangerous but he was bound to be less dangerous without a gun.

17.

The resort was deserted. They ran into the reception area but found no one. The giant shipwreck painting now served as a perfect metaphor for this trip.

"HELLO?" yelled Rob.

He picked up the phone and tapped the receiver several times.

"It's dead."

"Why isn't there anybody here?" Celeste asked in disbelief.

Rob scanned the reception wall and grabbed a copy of their room card. Rob had to know if his phone was still on the carpet where he had left it.

Out of sight.

Rob silently praised himself for hiding it from his girlfriend in the first place.

"Let's get the car and get out of here," said Celeste. "Do you still have a car key?"

"The spare key is stuck under the car in a magnetic box."

Celeste took Rob's hand and they headed out the door towards their car.

"I've never been so glad that you do things like that," Celeste said as they ran. "Let's hurry."

Rob put the key in the ignition but the car made no sound. He had no real mechanical knowledge and knew that if he popped the hood it would be a waste of time. He concluded that Gordon probably did something to their car while they were trapped in the cave. He had seen what kind of car they were driving at reception that first day and there were no other guests at the resort.

"What now?" Celeste asked.

"We can't get away."

He's going to find us.

Celeste had looked at the map to Lake Cook resort multiple times. She was struggling to recall it now but was fairly certain it had only one main entrance.

"I think that's the only road."

"We could run... but we might..." Rob's voice faded off as he spoke. Celeste could tell he didn't want to think about what might happen if Gordon caught them. Neither of them had really had a chance to process the events from the cave. As they sat in the quiet of the car they were both starting to see the faces of the dead hikers. It was a horrid image and Rob shook it from his mind.

Gordon is coming. Think fast.

"Look, I have the other key to our room," he said holding up the room card. "We could barricade ourselves in there."

"We could get trapped."

"I didn't want to say anything before, but I left my phone in the bedroom."

Celeste started nodding. Any plan was better than no plan right now.

"It's probably still plugged in on my side of the bed. We can call for help if I can get a signal."

"Gordon would have grabbed it."

"I hid it on the floor."

"I don't know..."

Celeste's eyes darted around the car. Rob could see the distress in her face growing and tried to calm her down.

"Look, if you want to run, we'll run" he said as he took her hand.

His steadiness seemed to absorb the fear from Celeste.

"No," she said, "we can't keep running. Let's go to the room."

"You're sure?"

"We don't have time to argue, let's go."

In the distance Gordon watched them get out of the car and start running. He followed them but they dropped out of sight. As he approached the cabins he stopped and listened.

They must have gone into one of these doors he thought *but which one?*

He slowly crept forward and listened again. The air was filled with sounds from nature. Gordon didn't think he had been spotted so he continued his search in silence. Mere metres away Rob and Celeste had entered their room and Rob had rushed upstairs to his phone. He picked it up and tapped it vigorously without response. It was flat!

Shit. Fuck. Balls.

He traced the cord to the wall and saw that in his sleepy state he hadn't turned on the charger. His face fell as he turned to Celeste.

"No good," he managed to say, hoping that would be enough.

They wouldn't have time to charge the phone.

Gordon must be close. He'll find us.

Rob clicked the power on and they walked out into the living room. Celeste saw something that made her scream, giving away their position.

Gordon turned on the spot and headed for their door.

Room 14.

"Hello? Celeste honey?" called Gordon through the door.

Celeste had stumbled upon the body of Thomas. His dead eyes stared back at her in frozen agony. A large shard of glass was still wedged firmly in his side and Rob concluded from the impossibly large stain that he had probably bled to death. Celeste was unable to move. She started to cry. She was certain that Gordon had done this. Thomas was innocent and this death was a horrible sight. Three innocent people had now died. Gordon bashed his hands on the door again.

"Gordon, leave us alone!" yelled Rob.

"You seem like a nice guy Rob but nice guys never get the girl," said Gordon hoping to provoke Rob into a fight.

"You're a lunatic!" he shot back. Rob moved Celeste away from Thomas' lifeless body.

"Let me in!"

"Just leave me alone!" cried Celeste. "Why did you kill him Gordon?"

"Who?" Gordon was confused.

"Thomas, the owner. What's *wrong* with you?"

Gordon suddenly felt a wave of regret. *Thomas was dead?* He hadn't intended to kill him and had put their altercation out of his mind. He remembered telling him all about Celeste when he'd first started working at the resort. Thomas had been kind to him and given him a job and a chance to forget his troubles. Then from out of nowhere Gordon thought about Gwen.

"You're a monster," shouted Celeste.

He had passed the point of no return. He was responsible for all of this. It had to end today. He shook his head and pretended he hadn't killed Thomas. He closed his eyes and decided he wasn't the cause of either death in the cave.

Reset.

Gordon was focussed. This would all be in vain if he allowed Celeste and Rob to be together. Stopping their love was a cause worth fighting for.

Worth dying for.

"Last chance Celeste!" he screamed.

"She doesn't love you," Rob said as he started walking towards the door.

"I love Rob," Celeste chimed in. Rob appreciated her input. He had only just realised how much he was now shaking. Rob was taking charge. It was the first time he had needed to in his life.

He's so good in a crisis Celeste thought proudly.

There was silence on the other side of the door. Gordon had started walking away.

Where is he?

"I think he's gone," said Rob, "but he'll be back."

"What should we do?" asked Celeste. She was out of ideas and since Rob had brought them back to the room she was happy enough for him to get them out again. She didn't want to confess that she had no idea what she was doing anymore.

"Well we can't risk staying here... he could be getting a crowbar or a spare set of keys or anything." Rob took hold of Celeste by both shoulders as he revealed his plan.

"We have to swim for it."

"What?"

Across the lake.

Rob could see Celeste was shocked at the suggestion but it was the best plan Rob could come up with. All those lunchtimes at the pool were about to pay off. They moved to the balcony where they had eaten dinner together only two nights earlier. If Rob and Celeste could swim across Lake Cook then they might be able to escape from Gordon. It was a dash through the tree line and then mostly downhill away from the resort.

"We could make it... I don't want you to get hurt though. It looks shallow."

Celeste nodded.

She looked out over the water and felt a wave of vertigo strike her.

"I'm scared."

Rob tried to be supportive and gave Celeste a quick back rub. He thought about pushing her over the edge. Tough love had never been his strong suit and he dismissed the idea. Rob threw his legs over the balcony and paused.

"I'll go first," he said smiling at Celeste. She didn't smile back.

"Looks like we might have time for activities after all," he joked. Trying to lighten the mood was useless, as she stood almost motionless.

"Do you trust me?" he asked.

"Yes of course."

It was the only plan.

We can't stay here.

"Then follow me," said Rob as he dropped into the water like a pin. The cold water shocked his system as he broke the surface. It wasn't too shallow and for a moment he felt justified choosing this course of action. From the water Rob could see Gordon several hundred metres away. He looked back up at Celeste and then again at Gordon. He was rummaging through an old metal chest and kneeling on the gravel. He hadn't noticed Rob's escape attempt at all.

What's he doing?

"Come on Celeste, quickly!" Rob called up as quietly as he could.

Don't draw attention to yourself Rob.

They would have to be quick but Rob was becoming confident they *could* slip away undetected.

Celeste nodded and put one of her legs over the balcony railing. Rob could see she was shaking but he tried to be optimistic.

You can do this.

Celeste looked down at him. He waved his hand, motioning for her to jump.

A leap of faith.

Rob turned his attention back to Gordon and saw something that filled him with dread. Gordon had pulled a shotgun from the metal chest and was loading it with bullets. Rob's eyes went wide and he called up to Celeste.

"You have to jump now Celeste."

Celeste didn't move.

Jump Celeste.

Nothing. She wasn't jumping.

"He's got a shotgun!" yelled Rob.

Gordon heard him.

Shit.

Gordon finished loading the gun and started to jog towards the door of their room. Rob felt useless bobbing in the lake and looked up at Celeste.

Just jump. Please.

She shook her head as if to say 'I can't do this' and moved herself away from the edge.

In his disbelief Rob had no words. He floated alone in Lake Cook as Celeste went back into their room and out of his sight. There was nothing more Rob could do. He could hear them shouting back and forth through the door. He wondered whether he should be making a break for it. Was this her strategy? To buy him time to escape? The spontaneous trip to the mountains had done nothing for their relationship. Rob still had no idea what Celeste wanted and even less idea what she was thinking.

Maybe she wants Gordon he thought to himself.

Rob started floating backwards with the flow of the water. Moving away from the shouting wasn't his initial plan but he found himself unwilling to fight the current. He felt weak. There was no sign of Celeste or Gordon but he could hear them shouting in the distance. It wasn't until he heard the shotgun fire that he knew which direction to swim.

18.

Rob gasped for breath as he swam freestyle towards land. The surge of adrenaline had his body working at its peak. He pulled himself out of the water and pressed his hair back and out of his eyes.

Don't let her be dead he thought over and over again as he made his way towards the doorway.

Don't let her be dead.

Tears found their way down his face as he saw Celeste lying on the floor. She had a bloodied abdomen and was motionless.

Dead.

Gordon had shot their door open and it was missing a large piece. Shards of the door were scattered throughout the entrance. Gordon was a mess. He was on the floor crying next to Celeste, and still clutching his shotgun.

"What did you do?" managed Rob.

Dead.

He and Gordon were suddenly one in their shared grief. Celeste was dead and neither of them knew what to do next. This had become the worst moment in Gordon's life. The silence was deafening.

"I didn't mean to kill her. It was an accident."

"You shot her!" shouted Rob as he wiped away tears. He felt instant regret that he wasn't there for her.

The image of Celeste shaking her head at him from that balcony was burned into his mind. Why didn't she jump? He stared at her eyelids and began to cry at the thought of them never opening again.

Gordon tightened his grip on the shotgun and tried to stop himself from crying.

"She was meant to be with me. Are you happy now Rob?"

Rob was a broken man. It had taken her death for him to appreciate what they had together. He didn't care what happened next.

"What did she say to you Gordon... before she died?"

Rob held his breath and waited for an answer.

"She said that she was sorry. She told me that it might not seem like it right now but that there would be other girls."

Rob placed one hand on the doorway for support. He felt sick.

"I asked her why we couldn't be together. I told her that... she'd promised me we would always be together," Gordon said in a low voice.

Always. Rob remembered the inscription on the ring.

"It's too late now," said Rob. Gordon repositioned himself on the floor and continued.

"Celeste told me she loved you. You made her happy. That made me... angry... and I..." his eyes were still with disbelief. "... I shot the door open."

Gordon stopped talking as the memory flashed across his face.

You killed her.

"She was meant to be with me..." Gordon spoke suddenly. He stared at Rob with such sincerity that for a moment he agreed. If Gordon loved Celeste so much – enough to do all this – maybe Rob *should* have stepped aside. If he had Celeste might still be alive.

"It's over now," replied Rob between audible sobs. He slid himself to the floor and leaned against the damaged door.

They were two grown men crying over the death of a loved one. They both sat in slumped positions, unable to stand on their own. Gordon placed his hand on top of Celeste's and casually pointed the shotgun at Rob.

"When I bought Celeste an engagement ring I was so excited that I proposed that night. I wanted to do something special... something memorable but I couldn't wait. I had to be engaged to her straight away."

I was so impulsive. Why did I have to rush everything? Gordon thought to himself.

"I should have waited longer. We had dinner... we watched TV. Out of nowhere I proposed. I should have waited... and planned something special."

She deserved something special.

Rob stared at the opening at the end of the shotgun and imagined how easily it could all end.

"I killed her. That's what I did! It was an accident but *I* killed her."

Gordon left Celeste's hand alone and stood up. Rob and Gordon locked eyes. Rob knew in that moment that he didn't care if Gordon shot him right now. He didn't care about anything.

"Did you really love her Rob?"

He didn't hesitate to respond.

"I loved her, and I always will." Rob said.

Finish it Gordon.

Both men had the remnants of tears streaked down their faces. It was an unwinnable war now. The prize was gone. Gordon smiled at Rob and nodded. There was nothing left to say. He took the shotgun, placed it underneath his well-defined chin and pulled the trigger, killing himself instantly.

19.

Blood and brains were splattered across the room. Gordon's unrecognisable corpse had fallen forward in a heap and was now pooling blood in front of Rob. There were now three different blood types in the room. Rob was in complete shock. The shotgun blast was still ringing through his head as he tried to stand.

They're all dead.

This trip to Lake Cook resort had been the worst of his life. He stepped around Gordon towards his girlfriend.

Ex-girlfriend.

She had some blood across her face and as Rob moved to wipe it Celeste opened her eyes. She sat up suddenly and hugged Rob so tightly that he tumbled to the floor in confusion.

She's alive?

"Oh my God Rob..." Celeste shrieked loudly. "We're alive."

"I... Celeste?" was all he could manage.

How?

"I'm ok. I'm fine."

Celeste lifted her shirt to reveal her abdomen. It was stained with the same ink residue that Rob had on his fingers. He looked down and noticed the quill and empty inkpot on the floor for the first time.

"I was pretending," she explained. "I didn't think he would really kill me but when I saw the inkpot I had the idea."

Rob caught another glimpse of Gordon's remains and had to look away. He realised Celeste had been avoiding looking as well.

"Gordon told me to stand back from the door because he was going to shoot it open. I just knew I could use the ink and..."

"...I can't believe this," interrupted Rob.

Celeste still had blood on her face so he wiped it clean. Rob worried that this image would stay with him and that he would be forever changed by this moment. He could imagine the rest. Celeste had poured the dark ink onto herself and when the door was opened she would have faked her own death in front of Gordon. It must have been horrible for him to think he'd killed the woman he'd claimed to love so dearly.

She's alive.

Rob didn't know why, but he had started to cry. Celeste assumed the tears were for her and held him to her breast.

"It's okay Rob. It's all going to be alright."

"You scared me," he said. Rob had brought half the lake back with him and was suddenly conscious that he was getting everything in the room wet. He started to back out of the doorway and Celeste followed him carefully. Her eyes remained fixed on Rob, preventing her ever seeing what became of her ex-fiancé. Almost to compensate for her lack of interest Rob found he couldn't stop staring at Gordon. Until this weekend he had never seen a dead body. Now he had seen so many that he felt nothing. Gordon didn't deserve to die like that. He felt a momentary pang of hatred for the way Celeste had tricked him. She had tricked him with Gwen and now she'd tricked him into suicide.

Fool me once, shame on you. Fool me twice, shame on me.

20.

The interrogation was finally over and Wilkins and Lawsov seemed pleased with themselves. Rob knew he hadn't done anything wrong and something told him that he was about to be released.

"Just like I told you."

"It's nice to be so... innocent... in all this," said Lawsov with a smirk on his face.

"I *am* innocent."

Rob reclined in his chair and shook his right leg awake.

"Are we done?" he asked.

"Tell me something Rob," started Wilkins. "If your girl hadn't faked her death and Gordon *had* killed her... what then?"

His eyes lit up when he used the word 'killed' in an unexpected way.

"I don't think Gordon would have killed her."

"Let's just say he did."

Rob shook his head in disbelief. He was now fielding hypothetical questions too.

"Well, if he'd killed her then he probably would have killed me next."

Lawsov leaned against the wall.

"What about if he had killed her *accidently*?"

Rob shook his head as Lawsov continued.

"What if Gordon had shot your girlfriend... dropped the gun in despair and then you come in and suddenly you've got the gun..." Lawsov held an imaginary gun at Rob as he trailed off.

"I would have killed him."

"That's all I wanted to hear," smiled Lawsov.

I'm done.

Wilkins stood and opened the door to the interrogation room.

"Well Rob... you're free to go for now." Rob hadn't realised how dark it was in that small space until the door let excess light in.

"Celeste as well?"

"Of course," said Lawsov. "Gordon was the guilty one, right?"

Lawsov must have been absent the day they taught subtlety at the academy. His scepticism had made Rob nervous but he was so keen to get out of there that he refused to challenge it. Rob walked out the door and into a maze of corridors. He was led to the reception where Celeste stood waiting.

How long has she been out here? He hugged her close.

She wore the same blood and ink stained clothes as the last time they had been together.

They had been separated almost immediately and seeing her again made him relax a little more.

"Like I said, you're free to go" said Wilkins. The policemen watched Rob collect his bag from reception and move towards the exit.

"Hey Rob?" called Lawsov.

Rob turned around to face the men.

"Don't leave town or anything."

Outside the police station Celeste was disturbed by the silence. She was filled with questions about his interrogation and whether it was all over now.

"Rob?" she prompted.

"Are you alright?" he replied.

"Yeah."

He believed her. Maybe by not looking at his dead body this event could be forgotten by Celeste and she could move on with her life. Maybe they could be happy again.

"Are we alright?" she asked Rob.

"Yeah," he replied.

She wasn't convinced at all.

21.

It had been months since Gordon's death and the two had rarely spoken about it. It had bothered Celeste at first that Rob wouldn't discuss it but she came to realise that it was his way of dealing with it all. Despite their enthusiasm Wilkins and Lawsov hadn't been in contact with them about the case, which made them assume it was closed. Rob had gone through a myriad of emotions when they got home. He questioned whether he could continue his relationship with Celeste at first but somehow this shared experience had brought them closer. Their relationship was damaged but hadn't been broken. Their one-year anniversary was just around the corner. Rob now sat at a crossroads. He had decided that he loved Celeste and wanted to marry her. It was the right thing to do. That afternoon he sat on their brown sofa staring at a brand new engagement ring. His phone rang, as though Celeste instinctively knew what he was up to.

"Hello?"

"Hi honey it's me."

Celeste had been nothing but amazing for the last few weeks. She had been quick to laugh at his jokes, kept their apartment clean and made Rob feel so safe and happy. She was calling now to see what he wanted for dinner.

"So, when do you think you'll be home?" Rob asked while admiring the ring.

"It's a busy one! Might be a bit late. I've just got this meeting in the city in ten minutes and then I'll get some takeaway if you want?"

"Sounds good."

Celeste had painted a series of pictures based on their capture and the media exposure had guaranteed they sold. For the first time in a long time she was the breadwinner. Rob had taken annual leave and was enjoying not being at work. His time at Lake Cook had changed his perspective and work had started to take a backseat to life. This change in priorities had led to a new era of happiness. By being home more often he had started to notice little things about Celeste that he loved. He found her minutiae fascinating.

"What do you feel like?"

"How about you decide?" he replied.

"It doesn't matter to you?"

Celeste had been trying to let Rob make his own decisions lately.

"I'm not fussy."

"How about Thai food?" she offered.

They hadn't eaten satay chicken since that night at the resort and neither felt game enough to mention it. Celeste knew that he loved Thai food and was not surprised with his response.

"Good! I'll see you tonight then?"

"Can't wait."

"I Love you Rob."

"Love you too."

Rob smiled to himself and imagined her saying yes.

Yes.

As he put the engagement ring back into its box it slipped and bounced under the sofa. Rob reached down, searching for it. His fingers brushed against a foreign object and curiosity led him to investigate. The engagement ring was leaning against a small velvet box that Rob had never seen before. He put the ring away safely and placed the box on the sofa.

What the hell is this?

It wasn't locked but had a small metal latch keeping it closed. He had to open it. Inside the small box were letters, photos and jewellery.

Mementos.

He looked at the photos first and saw a different man in each picture. The only thing they had in common was that they all seemed to be happy. In one picture you could see a woman's hand in the foreground. Rob couldn't be sure but he thought it might have been Celeste's hand. Who were these men?

Did Celeste take these pictures?

His eyes were drawn to the engagement ring on her finger. The final photo was one of Gordon and

Celeste. He was wearing a Christmas jumper and had his arm around her. Celeste was staring up at him lovingly while he laughed at something happening behind the camera. Rob couldn't move. He had never been exposed to her past like this. She looked so at ease with Gordon. Why was she keeping this? Why did she have *any* of this? He was annoyed. How could he propose to her now?

More secrets and more lies.

Before he could look at the first letter there was a knock at the door. Rob was startled and quickly put the photos back in their velvet coffin. He slid the box back under the sofa and made his way to the door.

Who could that be?

Standing on the other side of their door was a woman with a pair of stunning green eyes. She had long brown hair and could have been a model on any catwalk around the world. She wore a tight dress that drew attention to her chest – which is exactly where Rob found himself staring. She was breathtaking.

"Can I help you?"

She smiled and tucked her hair behind her ear.

"I'm Gwen."

Gwen was even more attractive than he'd imagined.

Note from the Author.

In 2006 it was my pleasure to see my screenplay 'The Last Resort' turned into a feature length film. We made the film independently in Canberra, Australia on a small budget, which meant we were restricted in what we could and couldn't achieve. I love the fact that we made a feature film and I enjoyed most of the process.

In the years since the film was released, however, it has bothered me that certain elements of the story – including my original ending – were never fully realised. Part of the reason was compromise. As the Director I made the choice of a beautiful and very accommodating resort venue at the cost of some narrative elements. If you've read the novel you may have concluded, as I did, that some of the visuals that take place during the climactic scenes in Room 14 would be difficult to achieve without destroying property and creating quite a mess. The images of death may have become associated with the venue, which was understandably a difficult scenario for a working business.

The compromise changed the film. Some elements became better – such as an escape on canoes and a chase through wilderness. Others strayed from the original vision of my screenplay.

No-one is really to blame for any of this and given more money and time I'm still not sure we would have made the same film that I dreamed up to begin with. This was my first film after all.

It was simply a *different* ending than my original vision. At the end of the day there was a part of me that wanted to finish the story once and for all and I feel I have done that here. This novel represents the most accurate version of The Last Resort. This is the story I would have told if there were no limitations on me as a first time Director, on finances and on time.

I'm proud of the work we did, and a film isn't made by one person. I have to thank the Producers, my wonderful cast and the hard working crew for helping me realise a personal dream.

This narrative is dedicated to you all.

David Farrell

About the Author

David Farrell lives in Melbourne

with his wife Tess & their children.

He is a former Projectionist and has Directed two feature
films: The *Last Resort* & *The Young and The Wrestlers*.

Both are available to watch for free on YouTube.

David also has a film Podcast called *Pod Me If You Can*.

Look out for his other novels

The Glove, Twelve, Twelve More & *Dropping the Belt.*

@DaveFarrell1 on Twitter

Become a fan of The Last Resort at

www.facebook.com/LastResortFilm

www.ingramcontent.com/pod-product-compliance
Lightning Source LLC
Chambersburg PA
CBHW070012140726
47908CB00020B/1274